Other Yearling Books You Will Enjoy

The Penderwicks by Jeanne Birdsall
The Penderwicks on Gardam Street by Jeanne Birdsall
How Tía Lola Came to ~~Visit~~ Stay by Julia Alvarez
How Tía Lola Learned to Teach by Julia Alvarez
When You Reach Me by Rebecca Stead
Babe by Dick King-Smith
Ballet Shoes by Noel Streatfeild
Gifts from the Sea by Natalie Kinsey-Warnock
Holes by Louis Sachar
Little Joe by Sandra Neil Wallace

Nancy AND PLUM

Betty MacDonald

Illustrated by Mary GrandPré

with an introduction by Jeanne Birdsall

A Yearling Book

Text copyright © 1952 by Betty MacDonald, copyright renewed 1980 by Anne Elizabeth Evans and Joan Keil
Introduction copyright © 2010 by Jeanne Birdsall
Cover art and interior illustrations copyright © 2010 by Mary GrandPré

All rights reserved. Published in the United States by Yearling, an imprint of Random House Children's Books, a division of Random House, Inc., New York. Originally published in the United States with different illustrations by J. B. Lippincott, Philadelphia, in 1952, and subsequently published in hardcover in the United States by Alfred A. Knopf, an imprint of Random House Children's Books, New York, in 2010.

Yearling and the jumping horse design are registered trademarks of Random House, Inc.

Visit us on the Web! www.randomhouse.com/kids

Educators and librarians, for a variety of teaching tools, visit us at www.randomhouse.com/teachers

The Library of Congress has cataloged the hardcover edition of this work as follows:
MacDonald, Betty Bard.
Nancy and Plum / by Betty MacDonald ; illustrated by Mary GrandPré. — 1st Alfred A. Knopf ed.
p. cm.
Summary: Two orphaned sisters are sent to live at a boarding home run by the cruel and greedy Mrs. Monday, where they dream about someday having enough to eat and being able to experience a real Christmas.
ISBN 978-0-375-86685-2 (trade) — ISBN 978-0-375-96685-9 (lib. bdg.) — ISBN 978-0-375-89776-4 (ebook)
[1. Orphans—Fiction. 2. Sisters—Fiction. 3. Boardinghouses—Fiction.] I. GrandPré, Mary, ill. II. Title.
PZ7.M1464Nan 2011
[Fic]—dc22
2009039778

ISBN 978-0-375-85986-1 (pbk.)

Printed in the United States of America

10 9 8 7 6 5 4 3 2 1

First Yearling Edition 2011

Random House Children's Books supports the First Amendment and celebrates the right to read.

For Anne and Joan

Introduction

ONCE THERE WAS a young girl named Betty who enjoyed making up stories to tell her sister Mary at bedtime. The stories were about two other sisters, Plum and Nancy. Unlike Betty and Mary, who had a big, happy, safe family, Plum and Nancy were orphans who had wild adventures, like escaping from their terrible orphanage, being kidnapped by bank robbers, and stowing away on a boat to China.

The bedtime tales about the orphan sisters went on for years, but Betty couldn't help growing up, and when she did, she got married, moved away from home, and, sometime later, became an author. Her first book, *The Egg and I*, was for adults, and was so well written and funny that it made her famous. Much encouraged, Betty went on to write more books for adults, and also some for children—all about Mrs. Piggle-Wiggle, who knew everything there is to know about being young, was as wise as she was happy and as magical as she was commonsensical, and always had delicious snacks on hand for visitors.

Through all of this writing, Betty never forgot those old bedtime stories about orphans, and eventually she put a version of them into a book called *Nancy and Plum*. The kidnapping bank robbers and the boat to China are gone, but the sisters still live in a terrible orphanage. It's run by Mrs. Monday, who is "as warm and motherly as a pair of pliers," or, in other words, not at all like the wondrous Mrs. Piggle-Wiggle. Mrs. Monday's horrid little niece, Marybelle, lives there, too, spying and tattling and threatening the unwary with recitations of Longfellow. Then there are the other orphans, a sad and lonely lot, who look to Nancy and Plum for comfort and leadership. And who wouldn't? The sisters are charmingly self-sufficient. They can roast potatoes in wood-stoves and make a doll out of burlap sacks. They can scrub floors, cut lawns, trim hedges, and weed gardens. When they're locked up without food, they climb out a window and run to the barn for fresh milk. When they can't mail letters the normal way, they use a chicken for a carrier pigeon. And when Mrs. Monday and Marybelle become too evil to bear, Nancy and Plum escape from the orphanage with the help of everyone from an old horse named Jerry to a friendly librarian named Miss Appleby to a kindly farmer named Campbell.

Though I never heard the original stories, I don't regret

losing the bank robbers, et cetera, because for me, *Nancy and Plum* is perfect just as it is. I'm guessing Betty's sister Mary, who did hear the originals, thought the same. But I do wonder if Mary ever complained that Betty, who was the younger sister of the two, gave all the best lines to Plum, the fictional younger sister. While the swashbuckling Plum gets to say things like "I wish I had some firecrackers, I'd take out all the powder and blast my way out," Nancy, the timid one, is stuck saying "How can Plum be so brave?" I choose to imagine that if Mary did complain, Betty told her to write her own books. Which Mary did, but those details are for a different introduction.

In this tale I'm telling of sisters, there is yet one more set to consider. Before Betty wrote any of her books, she had two daughters. And these daughters must have been just as important to *Nancy and Plum* as Mary and Betty were, or even Nancy and Plum, because Betty said so right there on the dedication page. Read it for yourself. It says: "For Anne and Joan."

Three pairs of sisters, woven together through time and stories—this is *Nancy and Plum*. Enjoy.

Jeanne Birdsall
Author of *The Penderwicks*

1

Mrs. Monday's Boarding Home

IT WAS CHRISTMAS EVE. Big snowflakes fluttered slowly through the air like white feathers and made all of Heavenly Valley smooth and white and quiet and beautiful. Tall fir trees stood up to their knees in the snow and their outstretched hands were heaped with it. Trees that were bare of leaves wore soft white fur on their scrawny, reaching arms and all the stumps and low bushes had been turned into fat white cupcakes. Mrs. Monday's big brick Boarding Home for Children wore drifts on its window sills, thick frosting on its steep slate roofs, big white tam o'shanters on its cold chimneys and by the light of the lanterns on either side of the big iron gates you could see that each of the gateposts wore a round snow hat. Even the sharp spikes of the high iron fence had been blunted by the snow.

However, in spite of its snowy decorations, in spite of the beauty of its setting, and even in spite of its being Christmas Eve, Mrs. Monday's was a forbidding-looking establishment. The fences were high and strong, the house was like a brick fortress and the windows, with the exception of one small one high up and almost hidden by the bare branches of a large maple tree, were like dark staring eyes. No holly wreath graced the heavy front door, no Christmas-tree lights twinkled through the windows and beckoned in the passer-by, no fragrant boughs nor pine cones were heaped on the mantel of the large cold fireplace, for Mrs. Monday, her niece Marybelle Whistle and all but two of her eighteen boarders had gone to the city to spend Christmas. Nancy and Plum Remson (Plum's real name was Pamela but she had named herself Plum when she was too little to say Pamela), the two boarders who remained, were left behind because they had no mother and father. No other place to go on Christmas Eve.

You see, six years before, when Nancy and Plum were four and two years old, their mother and father had been killed in a train wreck and the children turned over to their only living relative, one Uncle John, an old bachelor who lived in a club in the city, didn't know anything about children, didn't want to know anything about children and did not like children. When the telegram from the Remsons' lawyer came notifying Uncle John of the tragic accident and the fact that he had just inherited two little girls, he was frantic.

"Dreadful!" he said, fanning himself with his newspaper.

"Gallivanting around the country getting killed. Dreadful and careless! Two little children! Heavens! What will I do with them? I'll have to move from this nice leather chair in this nice comfortable club and will probably wind up washing dishes and making doll clothes. Dreadful! Heavens!" Beads of sweat sprang out on his forehead like dew and he fanned himself some more. It was while he was folding his newspaper to make a bigger and better fan that he noticed the advertisement. It read:

CHILDREN BOARDED—Beautiful country home with spacious grounds, murmuring brooks, own cows, chickens, pigs, and horses. Large orchard. Delicious home-cooked food. A mother's tender loving care. Year round boarders welcome. Rates upon request. Address Mrs. Marybelle Monday, Box 23, Heavenly Valley.

With trembling hands, Uncle John tore out the advertisement and wrote a letter to Mrs. Monday. He received an immediate answer and three days later he was on his way to inspect this delightful boarding home so chock-full of good food and tender loving care for little children.

It was springtime in Heavenly Valley and the fields were golden with dandelions, the slopes were foaming with cherry blossoms, the sky was lazily rolling big white clouds around and meadowlarks trilled in the thickets. Uncle John was entranced. "Had forgotten the country was so beautiful!" he said to his chauffeur. "Certainly the place for children. Beautiful, beautiful!"

When they drew up to the imposing entrance of Mrs. Monday's Boarding Home for Children, Uncle John was most impressed. "Nice, solid, respectable place," he said, noting the very large, sturdily built brick house surrounded by the high spiked iron fence. "Well built," he said to his chauffeur, who had jumped out to open the heavy iron gates for him.

"It certainly is," the chauffeur said, wondering to himself why a boarding home for little children should have such a wicked-looking fence. Surely not just to keep the rolling lawns from oozing out into the road!

Just then Mrs. Monday, who had been watching and waiting behind the curtains in her sitting room, came rushing out the front door, hands outstretched, thin mouth pulled apart in what was supposed to be a smile.

"My dear, dear, dear Mr. Remson," she gushed as Uncle John waddled up the walk. "Do come in. The dear little children and I have been waiting for you."

Uncle John shook one of her hands briefly and said, "Nice place. Well built."

Mrs. Monday said, "Well, I always say, dear Mr. Remson, nothing is too good for little children. Now," she said, piloting him into her sitting room, the only comfortable room in the large cold house, and settling him in an easy chair in front of the fireplace in which burned a nice cheerful little fire, "you must see my little ones. My little family!" She rang for Katie to bring tea and to summon the children. Happy at the prospect of a cup of hot tea and perhaps toast with raspberry jam, Uncle John waited.

The first to come, however, was not the tea tray but Mrs. Monday's niece, Marybelle Whistle, a most unattractive, doughy child with pale close-set eyes, a mouth like a mail slot and hundreds of grayish-white curls that exploded from her head like sausages. For the occasion she had been carefully dressed in a ruffly pink silk dress, pink silk socks and shiny new black patent-leather slippers. Certain that she looked adorable, Marybelle flounced up to Uncle John and announced in a high squeaky voice, "How do you do, Mr. Remson? I am Marybelle." Uncle John drew back with distaste and said, "Really!" Marybelle said, "Yes, and I am very smart and can recite 'The Children's Hour' all the way through, want to hear me?"

"Heavens, no!" said Uncle John so loudly and forcefully that Marybelle, who had already opened her mouth to begin, jumped back and almost fell in the fireplace. This naturally caused much merriment among the other children, who though vigorously scrubbed, combed and braided (even if they had curly hair) had been instructed to stay outside the door so that Uncle John wouldn't see their faded, patched clothing.

Uncle John, hearing their laughter and having no idea that he had been the cause of it, said, "Happy little things. Laughing children must be happy." Marybelle, who wasn't happy and wasn't laughing, sulkily left the room, and Uncle John, who didn't know that she was Mrs. Monday's niece, turned to Mrs. Monday, who was glaring at the children, and said, "Horrible, forward little creature. Must have dreadful

5

parents. I can't abide children who recite." This, of course, made the other children laugh so hard that Mrs. Monday got up and tersely ordered them to be quiet and go to their rooms. She then firmly shut the sitting-room door. Then Katie brought the tea and there were not only toast and raspberry jam but fresh hot cupcakes. Uncle John forgot about Marybelle and concentrated on the food and after a while he looked at Mrs. Monday and thought, "Fine woman. Taking care of other people's children. Fine woman!"

If he had had the sense of a rabbit, of course, or had known or cared anything about children, he would have noticed that this "fine woman" had large, cold, close-set eyes, a mouth that snapped shut like a purse, a smile that bared her large yellow teeth but did not light up her eyes, a voice that caused children to flinch and look frightened whenever she spoke to them and a general appearance about as warm and motherly as a pair of pliers. He would also have noticed that although Marybelle Whistle was well dressed, the other little boarders had sad hungry eyes, thin hungry bodies and ill-fitting, worn-out clothes.

But, as I have said, Uncle John didn't care about children and he was very anxious to get rid of Nancy and Plum, so he saw what he wished to see and didn't see what he didn't wish to see, and three days later he delivered his two little nieces and all of their belongings to Mrs. Monday. Since that day, as far as Nancy and Plum knew, he had not written or been to see them. He didn't know if they got his presents, which they didn't. Or if they were happy, which they weren't. He paid

Mrs. Monday handsomely for their board and room and clothing and Mrs. Monday wrote and told him how beautifully the children were growing and how happy they were. The two or three times Nancy and Plum had written to Uncle John, Mrs. Monday had found and burned the letters.

2

Christmas Eve

So here it was Christmas Eve and Uncle John was sitting in his club in the city drinking from the wassail bowl and talking to his old cronies and if he thought of Nancy and Plum at all, which I doubt, it was only to wonder if they were too old for the dolls he had sent them.

In Heavenly Valley, Nancy and Plum, who hadn't gotten the dolls, stood at the window of their cold, bare, little room straining their eyes through the snowflakes toward a far-off cluster of lights, like a handful of stars, that marked the schoolhouse where the Christmas Eve entertainment was being held.

Nancy said, "I wonder what time it is?"

Plum said, "About seven I guess. Mrs. Monday and the children took the six o'clock train."

Nancy said, "If it's seven, then they'll just be starting the carols at school."

Plum said, "And old Squeaky Swanson will be singing the solo you should be singing. When she gets to the 'Oh, Night Deeeeviiiiiine!' part she sounds like a screech owl, and anyway she doesn't look like an angel. She looks like a mouse in a white nightgown."

Nancy laughed and said, "Oh, Plum, poor old Muriel can't help the way she looks. Besides, you probably think I sing better because I'm your sister."

Plum said, "Squeaky can't help the way her face looks but she doesn't have to wear that long underwear and have those big knobby lumps on her knees and ankles. She knows very well that angels don't wear long underwear and anyway her mother makes so many mistakes when she plays her accompaniment that it always sounds as though she and Squeaky were on different songs."

Nancy said, "I wish we had a mother, even one like Mrs. Swanson."

Plum said, "If we had a mother, do you suppose we'd have to wear long underwear and be lumpy?"

Nancy said, "I can remember our mother a little bit and she was beautiful. I don't think she ever made us wear long underwear."

Plum said, "One thing about mothers, they might make you wear long underwear but they force the teachers to give you the best parts in the Christmas play."

Nancy said, "Our mother wouldn't have to. Miss Waverly likes us and she wanted us both in the play until Mrs. Monday told her we couldn't."

Plum said, "Miss Waverly thinks you sing a million, billion times better than old Squeaky Swanson, she told me so and she said that you'd make a beautiful angel with your red hair combed out and hanging down your back all bright and shining. . . ."

"And probably one of Mrs. Monday's gray flannel nightgowns flapping around my old worn-out shoes. Oh, Plum, wouldn't it be wonderful if we were in the Christmas play and we had white satin angel dresses with filmy white wings?"

Plum said, "I guess we'll have to wait until we get to heaven and are real angels. Didn't the Christmas tree look beautiful? I think Miss Waverly feels sorry for us and that is why she let us decorate it."

Nancy said, "As long as we are the only children who have no place to go for Christmas, I don't see why Mrs. Monday wouldn't let us go to the school entertainment. We could have walked and every child in the Valley is getting an orange, some candy and a gift."

Plum said, "Speaking of candy, I'm hungry. Let's go down to the kitchen and see if we can find anything to eat besides oatmeal."

Nancy said, "Oh, don't worry, she locked up everything but the prunes and the oatmeal. Oh, look down the road there, Plum. Two little lights and they're moving. It must be a sleigh. Someone going to the Christmas entertainment."

Plum said, "Quick, help me open the window so we can hear the bells."

They pushed open the window and leaned out into the still, cold night air. Far off down the road, through the lazily drifting snowflakes, they could hear the merry sound of sleigh bells. Their gay little tinkling flying ahead of the sleigh and lighting up the night with sparks. "Oh, what a Christmasy sound!" Nancy said, her red braids bobbing excitedly.

Plum said, "Let's run out to the gate and watch the sleigh pass."

"Oh, yes," Nancy said. "Here, I'll shut the window. Come on, hurry!"

Like little ghosts, they ran from their room, down the long, cold, dark corridor, down the long, dark winding stairway, across the drafty hall, out the front door and down the walk to the great iron gates.

Breathless and laughing, they grabbed the bars of the gates and turned their faces in the direction of the sleigh bells. Snowflakes lit on their eyelashes and made them blink. Snowflakes lit on their hair and turned them into white-haired old ladies. Snowflakes lit on their tongues when they stuck them out; and they swallowed the drop of icy water they left.

Nancy said, "Snowflakes are like tiny pieces of clouds. Maybe a cloud exploded and caused this snowstorm."

Plum said, "Everything is so soft tonight. The darkness, the air, the snow, everything. I'd like to throw myself down and make an angel." Above their heads the snow hit the lanterns on the gateposts and dissolved with a gentle hissing sound. The gate groaned sadly as they leaned against it.

Then, from down the road, came the shrill trilling of the sleigh bells, the thud of hooves, the *shshsh* of runners on snow, peals of laughter. Then suddenly as though they had leapt through a black curtain, the horses burst out of the snowy darkness, manes and forelocks crested with snow, heads high, eyes glowing like hot coals. For a moment they were so close the children could see their white breath and could smell their warm, horsy smell.

"Merry Christmas!" Plum called out excitedly.

"Merry Christmas!" Nancy echoed her, and voices in the sleigh answered, "Merry Christmas!" Then they were gone into the blackness again and nothing was left but the tinkling of the bells and the hiss of the snowflakes as they hit the lanterns.

"Oh, Plum," Nancy said, "imagine going to the Christmas Eve entertainment in a sleigh!"

Plum said, "Someday we'll go in a sleigh and I'll drive."

Nancy said, shivering, "Not tonight though, and I'm cold. Let's go back in the house."

So they ran up to the front door but when they turned the handle they found it locked. Locked tight.

"The night latch must have been on," Plum said, "and the rest of the house is locked up like a safe."

"What will we do?" Nancy asked through chattering teeth.

Plum said, "We'll sleep in the barn."

Nancy said, "But what about Old Tom?"

Plum said, "He's gone to the MacGregors' for supper. He

13

told me he was going yesterday when I was helping him feed the chickens. He's not coming back till milking time tomorrow morning. Come on, let's run. I've got snow down my neck and my feet are like ice."

They ran around the house, unlatched the lattice gate that shut off the kitchen gardens and stables from the front lawns, ran across the barnyard to the big red-brick barn, rolled back the door and slipped inside. The barn was very dark but not as cold as the house. They closed the door quickly and began to grope around for matches and a lantern. As they carefully felt along the shelves, they could hear Buttercup and Clover, the milk cows, chewing their cuds, the plow horses shifting their weight on their big feet, the pigs grunting in the box stall and mice scuttling around in the granary stealing the grain. They were friendly, comforting sounds, and Nancy said, "Even in the dark, the barn isn't nearly as lonely as the house."

Plum said, "I should say it isn't. I think I just grabbed hold of a mouse. Oh, here we are. Here's an old candle stub and some matches."

She struck a match and lit the candle. As the candle flame reached up and cast a circle of light, a black mother cat and three black kittens filed out of Buttercup's stall and came over to the little girls. "Mrooow," said the mother cat and the kittens squeaked, "Mrrow." Plum knelt down and stroked the mother, who rubbed against her legs and purred. Nancy went over and scratched Buttercup behind her horns and she licked Nancy's hand with her sandpaper tongue. Clover leaned out of her stall to see what was going on and as Nancy scratched her head, she stuck her tongue out about a foot and searched with the tip of it in the corners of her feed box for stray oats. Then Plum called out, "I found the lantern and it's full of coal oil. Here, hold the candle while I light it."

Both girls knelt down and worked with the lantern until they finally got the wick adjusted and the smoky chimney wiped off. The lantern gave quite a lot of light and they hung it on a nail while they patted the horses, poked the pigs and played with the kittens. Then Plum had an idea. She said, "Let's go in the harness room. There's a stove in there and we can build a fire and roast potatoes."

Nancy said, "Where'll we get the potatoes?"

Plum said, "From the root cellar. I know where it is and it's not locked because I helped Old Tom get apples one time!"

Nancy, who was shaking with the cold and very hungry, thought this sounded like a wonderful idea until they went into the harness room and found it tight against the storm but very harnessy smelling and quite chilly. "It's really nicer in the barn," she said.

But Plum, who had already opened up the door of the big black stove and was busily poking around in the ashes, said, "You just wait until I get this fire going. Oh, boy, here's some hot coals from Old Tom's milking-time fire. Hand me some of those shavings, will you, Nancy?"

Nancy did and Plum threw them in, tossed in some kindling and some lumps of coal and in no time had a bright crackling fire that blew its warm breath into the little girls' eager faces.

"Now that the fire's going," Plum said, rubbing her cold hands together, "let's go out to the root cellar."

"And," Nancy said, "then we can go to the milk room and get some milk and butter. Oh, this is going to be fun, Plum, and I'm so hungry."

"So am I," Plum said. "I'm starving and freezing. Let's hurry."

So, carefully shutting the door on the cat and her kittens, who had followed them into the harness room and intended to follow them everywhere they went, they ran through the barn and across the snowy barnyard to the root cellar. The root cellar, a little low house built into a bank by the back of the house, had a thick heavy door that was very hard to open but finally, after both girls had almost pulled their arms out of the sockets, they were able to squeeze through. It was very dark until Plum lit her candle stub and the air was pungent with the smells of the apples, carrots, potatoes, cabbages, squashes and rutabagas that were stored in the bins and shelves that lined the walls. The girls filled their aprons with four big potatoes, four dark red apples, some pears and a jar of peaches.

As she reached up to the high shelf where the canned fruit was kept, Nancy said, "I don't feel that it's wrong to take these peaches without asking because it is Christmas and everybody should have something special for Christmas dinner."

Plum said, "Of course Mrs. Monday's idea of something

16

special is fried mush or boiled beans with rocks in them. Say, let's take some carrots and apples for the animals. They'd like to have something special for Christmas, too."

So they added more things to their already bulging aprons. Apples for the horses, carrots for the cows and rutabagas for the pigs.

When they got back to the harness room the stove was blazing merrily and giving off so much heat that the cat and her kittens were stretched out on the floor in great comfort. Nancy and Plum washed the potatoes in the snow and put them in to roast, fed the animals their Christmas dinner, got butter and milk from the milk room, then settled down to enjoy themselves. First they took off their shoes and stockings and put them to dry, then sat down in front of the stove to thaw out their icy toes and fingers. Outside a wind had come up. It blew snow against the window and moaned and sighed in the eaves but the children played with the kittens and thought how cozy the wind sounded.

After the potatoes had been in about ten minutes, Plum began poking them with a sharp stick to test them and the minute she could pierce the skin she took the coal shovel and the poker and got out the first ones. They were really quite raw but they were hot and when covered with fresh butter and washed down with gulps of cold sweet milk they were simply delicious. The second potatoes were only raw in the middle and tasted even better than the first ones. For dessert the girls opened the jar of peaches with an old jackknife of Plum's and ate the peaches in their fingers in big bites.

"No wonder Mrs. Monday and Marybelle have peaches so often," Nancy said as she reached down inside the jar for the last one. "They are the best things I've ever tasted."

Plum said, in an imitation of Mrs. Monday, "My deah child, surely you don't prefer peaches to my delicious soggy bread pudding with glue sauce or my special kind of stewed prunes with sticks in them?"

Nancy said, "It isn't that I prefer the peaches, dear Mrs. Monday, it is just that after I have eaten your soggy, tasteless, lumpy, doughy lead, oh, I'm sorry, I mean bread pudding, I have to walk bent over for the rest of the day."

Plum said, "Would you like the recipe for my special prunes?"

Nancy said, "Oh, please."

Plum said, "Well, first you buy the tiniest, most dried up, most solid pit and skin prunes you can find, then you dump them into a huge kettle of water, about two prunes to a gallon of water, you never wash them first, of course, because the sticks and sand give them such a good flavor. Then you boil and boil and boil and boil them, add one teaspoon of sugar to each enormous kettle of juice and there you are. Stewed prunes à la Marybelle."

Nancy said, "Oh, look at the kittens. I think they are hungry."

Plum said, "Their saucer is in the barn. Hand me my shoes and I'll go get it."

After they had fed the kittens and picked up their own mess, Nancy and Plum made themselves a nice bed of straw spread over with empty feed sacks, stoked the fire, turned the lantern down and lay down side by side in front of the stove. The only sounds were the clunks and hisses made by coals breaking open and bursting into flame, the moaning of the wind and the rustling of the straw when they moved.

Nancy was watching the round glow of the lantern on the ceiling and thinking about the school entertainment when she heard a little sniff and a hot tear fell on her arm. She said, "Why, Plum, you're crying. That's not like you."

Plum said, "It's Christmas Eve and I hate Uncle John. He's supposed to take care of us and he never writes to us and he never comes to see us and he never even sends us Christmas presents. I wonder how he'd like to spend Christmas Eve eating raw potatoes and sleeping in a barn?"

Nancy said, "Never mind, Plum, dear. At least we're warm and we've had something to eat and I'll pretend for us."

Plum said, "Oh, Nancy, I'm sick of pretending. I don't think I can pretend any more."

Nancy said, "Well, I'm ten and you're only eight and pretending is easier for me, so I'll pretend out loud for both of us."

She began, "We live in a lovely little white house on a broad quiet street shaded with big trees. We have a beautiful mother, a handsome father and twin baby brothers, one for each of us. It is Christmas Eve and we have just decorated the Christmas tree. It is a very large tree and takes up lots of space in our living room but it is a pine with long needles and it smells so delicious that our mother says that it is well worth the space. Now that the tree is decorated, you and I go up-stairs and put on our white satin angel costumes with the silk gauze wings and our gold halos, then we all go to the school-house entertainment. Our mother and father are very proud of us because we sing all the Christmas carols for the whole school. We stand by the Christmas tree with a big spotlight on us and first I sing a solo and then you sing a solo and then we sing duets. When the spotlight first shines on us everybody in the schoolhouse just gasps, our costumes are so beautiful."

Plum said, "Who is going to play our accompaniments? Not Mrs. Swanson, I hope."

"Our mother plays our accompaniments," Nancy said. "She plays for all the school entertainments and she has never made one single mistake. After the Christmas entertainment is over, Miss Waverly distributes the gifts and she is certainly surprised to find a huge package for her from you and me."

"What's in the package?" Plum asked.

"Violet perfume, violet toilet water, violet powder, violet bath powder, violet bath salts and violet soap and there is a bunch of real violets tied to the outside of the package," Nancy said.

Plum said, "Just like that picture we cut out of the maga-zine. I bet Miss Waverly never had such a beautiful present. Why don't we ask her to our house for Christmas dinner?"

Nancy said, "Oh, that's a good idea, especially as I know how sad Christmas is at the Wentils' where she boards be-cause Charlie Wentil told me that his father believes that

Christmas trees or holly or any kind of Christmas presents are wicked and signs of the devil. Charlie told me that last year they all had to pray straight through from milking time to lunch because Charlie brought home a piece of tinsel from school and put it around the clock on the mantel."

Plum said, "I guess right now we're probably having twice as much fun as Charlie Wentil. Oh, look, Nancy, here come the kittens. They want to get in bed with us. Let's name them and pretend they belong to us. They can be our Christmas present. Let's name the mother St. Nick and the children Prancer, Dancer and Vixen."

Nancy said, "Those are good names, Plum. Here, St. Nick. Bring your children over here. We'll be gentle to them."

So St. Nick came over and settled herself and her children on the straw bed between the two little girls and when they stroked her sleek black fur she purred loudly and rubbed against their hands. Then Plum said, "Go on, Nancy, pretend some more."

So Nancy said, "Well, after the Christmas entertainment is over we go home and after we have put our baby brothers to bed, we hang up our stockings and then we all sing Christmas carols. Our father sings off-key but he has such a nice loud voice we don't care. After the carols we turn off all the lights but the ones on the Christmas tree and then we gather around the fireplace and drink hot cocoa. It is snowing and very stormy outside but so Christmasy and cozy inside.

"Earlier today, you and I made mince pies and Christmas

cookies while mother stuffed the turkey. Tomorrow morning we will get up early and rush downstairs and there will be a crackling fire in the fireplace and our mother and father will hug us and say, 'Merry, merry Christmas,' and then we will start to open our bulging stockings and the heaps of presents under the tree. I have made mother a beautiful checked apron and you have embroidered her two guest towels. We have made the babies some stuffed animals and we have knitted our father some mufflers."

"Let's pretend we buy everything," said Plum. "I'm tired of all those old homemade things. Anyway, I make too many mistakes when I knit."

Nancy said, "All right, we'll buy the presents this year but I do think that we should earn our own money so that we won't be too big a burden on our parents."

Plum said, "I don't want to work. I want rich parents. I want a father who says, 'Here, Pamela, is a hundred dollars. Your allowance for the week.'"

Nancy said, "Oh, Plum, when you're that rich it takes all the joy out of pretending. I don't want to be rich. I just want to be happy."

Plum said, "All right, I won't be rich but I won't knit that old scarf. I'll give my father a spy glass. Then Christmas morning I can go up on the roof and look around and see what everybody in the neighborhood got for Christmas."

Nancy said, "Well, I'm going to knit him a scarf and then every time he wears it he'll think of me."

Plum said, "He certainly will when the wind whistles through all those holes where you dropped stitches."

Both girls laughed and then suddenly they were asleep and their dreams must have been sweet ones for the wind howled, the stove shifted its coal and the kittens woke up and began to play but they slept quietly.

3

What Was in the Box?

THEN IT WAS MORNING and Nancy and Plum woke to find Old
Tom building up the fire and Dancer, Prancer and Vixen playing tug of war with one of Nancy's red braids.

Plum said, "Merry Christmas, Tom!"

Old Tom said, "Whatcha doin' out here in the barn?"

Plum said, "We got locked out last night."

Old Tom said, "Why didn't you go home for Christmas—
why did you stay here?"

Plum said, "You know we always stay here for Christmas.
You know we haven't any place to go."

Old Tom said, "Hmmmmph!"

Nancy said, "Come on, Plum, let's go see if we can get in

the house. Perhaps if we had a ladder we could get in one of the upstairs windows."

Old Tom said, "Ladder out in the barn. Heavy. I'll carry it for you."

Plum said, "Thank you, Tom. Wow, I'm hungry."

Tom said, "Warm milk in the milk room. Tin dipper by the door."

So the girls ran into the milk room and drank several dippers of the warm fresh milk. Then feeling very frisky, they went out to see if they could find an unlocked window.

My, but it was a beautiful morning. The sky was clear as a lake and the snow, which the wind had heaped against the buildings and fences in great swoopy drifts, sparkled and glittered in the bright sunshine.

Nancy said, "Oh, if we only had a sled."

"And a place to slide," Plum said, looking around at the flat barnyard.

"Woodshed roof's a good place," Old Tom said from the doorway behind them. "If you had a couple of flat pans you could put the ladder against the woodshed, climb up, walk along the ridgepole, get in your pan, slide to the edge, then jump off in the deep drift."

"Where'd we get the pans?" Plum asked.

"Tin washbasin's just the thing," Tom said. "Several of them in the washroom off the kitchen."

"But how will we get into the kitchen?" Nancy asked.

"Trunk-room window always open," Old Tom said as he squeezed past them with a long ladder. "Here, you, Plum, follow me," he called as he ploughed through the deep snow on the north side of the house.

Both Plum and Nancy followed him but they could see why he had called Plum when they saw the tiny little window below which he placed the top rung of the ladder.

"Now go on up there and see if that little window won't open," he said to Plum as he lifted her up and set her on the ladder above the deep snowdrift. Plum went up the ladder as quickly and agilely as a monkey and when she got to the window Tom called, "It opens in, Plum. Push hard."

Plum pushed and pushed and finally the window opened so suddenly that she almost fell through it headfirst. When she had righted herself and had a good hold on the window sill, she turned and called down to Old Tom, "What's in this room? It's awfully dark."

Old Tom said, "Nothing in there but trunks and old boxes. The window's not far from the floor, you can go in headfirst."

So Plum did and the last they saw of her for some little time were her thin legs and worn-out shoes flailing the air as she squeezed headfirst through the tiny window. Old Tom carried the ladder around to the back again and put it against the woodshed, which was high at the ridgepole but sloped almost to the ground on one side.

"That would be a fine place to slide," Nancy told Old Tom and he said, "I used to slide there myself when I was a boy."

Nancy said, "Have you always lived here, Tom?" and he said, "There's Plum now. She's got the back door open so you'd better scoot inside and put on a coat and some overshoes."

27

Nancy ran up the back steps and across the porch and as soon as she was inside and the back door closed Plum said, "Nancy, hurry, come upstairs, I want to show you something."

"What is it?" Nancy asked.

"Just you wait," Plum said. "Just you wait and see." And she took Nancy's hand and yanked her up the stairs as fast as she could go.

The trunk room was on the third floor of the house, at the end of the servants' wing and next to the little stairway that led to the attic. There was a thick white candle in a saucer outside the door and when Plum had lighted it she opened the door and went in, motioning to Nancy to follow her. Nancy did, but was disappointed to see nothing but trunks and empty packing boxes. It was one of the packing boxes, however, which seemed to interest Plum so much.

"Come here," she said to Nancy, her voice shaking with excitement. "Look, just look at this," and she lowered the candle so that Nancy could see the label pasted on the outside of the packing box. The label read,

> To: *Miss Nancy and Miss Pamela Remson*
> *c/o Mrs. Marybelle Monday*
> *Mrs. Monday's Boarding Home for Children*
> *Heavenly Valley*

Plum said, "Look here at the date of the postmark—December 15. And now look inside."

Nancy looked. Inside the box was divided into two long

sections and about a foot from the end on each side were cardboard partitions with a half-moon-shaped piece cut out of each partition. "What do you suppose was in these boxes," she asked Plum.

Plum said, "Dolls. See that round cut out place is where their necks went and I examined the boxes and I found hair stuck to the sides of the box. See," and she held up some silky hairs. "Some blond, some black."

Nancy turned back the lid of the box and looked again. Sure enough it was addressed to Plum and her and it also said,

From: Mr. John Remson
      The Croquet Club
      Central City

"Why, Plum," Nancy said, and there were tears in her eyes. "Uncle John hasn't forgotten us and he did send us Christmas presents."

Plum said, "Yes, and what happened to them?"

Nancy knelt down on the floor beside the box and said, "Plum, just look how big these dolls were. Why, they must have been almost as big as real little children. If we had them, which color hair would you choose?"

Plum said, "I'd choose the yellow hair."

Nancy said, "Oh, I'm so glad because I'd like to have a doll with jet-black hair just like I've always dreamed of having. I wonder how they were dressed?"

Plum said, "Well, I examined the rest of the box very

carefully, that is what took me so long, but I can't find any other clues, so we'll have to pretend. I'll pretend that my doll was a cowgirl with real little cowboy boots and a holster around her waist."

Nancy said, "Well, I want Rebecca, I named her after Rebecca of Sunnybrook Farm, to be dressed entirely in pink. Pink silk underwear, pink silk petticoat, pink silk dress, pink velvet coat and hat trimmed in fur. Even pink shoes and stockings. Oh, my, but I love black hair and the color pink."

Plum laughed and said, "That's just because you have red hair. I'm going to name my doll Annie after Annie Oakley and I'm going to teach her how to shoot flies at a hundred yards and to lasso a mouse from a full gallop."

Nancy said, "Listen, I hear someone calling."

Plum went to the window and stuck her head out. In a minute she turned to Nancy and said, "It's Old Tom. He wants us."

"What shall we do about the box?" Nancy asked.

Plum said, "Let's carry it down and hide it under our bed and then we'll confront Mrs. Monday with it."

So they put the box under their bed and then went down to see what Old Tom wanted. He only wanted to tell them that he was going to MacGregors' for Christmas dinner and that Mrs. Monday was coming home on the four o'clock train. Nancy and Plum thanked him and waved good-bye and then went into the kitchen to see if they could find anything for breakfast. As they suspected, everything but the prunes and oatmeal had been locked up tight but when Nancy opened the back door to get some kindling off the back porch she was surprised to find a little pan of fresh brown eggs, a can of new milk, a pat of butter and a note scrawled on a piece of wrapping paper, "Merry Christmas—Old Tom."

Nancy and Plum built a roaring fire in the kitchen stove, fried the eggs in butter, made toast out of some stale bread they found in the breadbox and had the best breakfast they had tasted in years. When they finished they washed their dishes and put them away, put the rest of the eggs on to hard boil for lunch and banked the fire with coal. Then they went into the washroom and got two large tin basins, put on their coats, caps, mittens and galoshes and went out to try sliding on the woodshed roof.

Plum was the first one down. She sat in the basin, held her arms and legs out stiff and Nancy gave her a shove. Around and around she whirled, like a pinwheel, as she slid down the roof. Just at the bottom the pan hit a nail and stopped dead and Plum was dumped headfirst into the snowdrift.

Nancy had to climb down the ladder and jerk Plum out by her ankles but then they both climbed right back up and Nancy took a turn. She started farther over to avoid the nail and though she turned around a few times she was able to jump out at the bottom and land feet first in the snowdrift. Then Plum came down and landed right side up and then Nancy, and pretty soon they had a slick hard track and went so fast they could stay right in their basins and land with a spank on the snow.

My, it was fun and pretty soon it was lunch time and they

were very hungry and so they ran into the kitchen and ate their hard-boiled eggs and drank some milk and dried their mittens and then out they went again and slid and made angels in the snow until the sun started going down behind the barn and they were hungry again.

This time they went in the barn and ate their apples and winter pears and played with Prancer, Dancer and Vixen and St. Nick until they heard the whistle of the four o'clock train and knew it was almost time for Mrs. Monday and the children. Slowly, reluctantly they said good-bye to their kittens and closed the barn door, put away the tin basins, hung up their wet coats and mittens and went up to their room to wait for Mrs. Monday.

Pretty soon the front door slammed and up the stairs and down the long cold corridor trooped the returning boarders. Nancy and Plum ran to greet them and to see what they had gotten for Christmas, which in most cases wasn't much because children sent to board with Mrs. Monday were not the children of parents or relatives who cared about them.

The worst presents were Tommy Wolton's checkerboard but no checkers; David Hilton's two new suits of long underwear; Mary Burton's hand-me-down coat and moth-eaten muff; Eunice Haggerty's homemade rag doll with the face all bunched up near the forehead and short, very stiff, very stumpy arms and legs; Todd Weatherby's new toothbrush and chart to keep track of how many times he brushed his teeth, and little Sally Cedric's new gray-flannel petticoat.

The best presents were Allan Murphy's copy of *Tom Sawyer*

and *Gulliver's Travels*, which he said Plum and Nancy could borrow, and Evangeline Carter's giant candy cane, which she said she would share with everyone. The other children had been given small, cheaply made windup toys which were already broken, or merely candy and oranges which were already eaten.

The funny thing is that although Nancy and Plum had had no Christmas at all of any kind, they almost cried when they saw Todd Weatherby's toothbrush and David Hilton's long underwear. Nancy said she could fix Eunice Haggerty's hideous rag doll that looked, Allan said, as though she had just eaten a quince and had been run over by a train. Nancy said that she would rip out the old squinty face and during next sock-darning session when Mrs. Monday and Marybelle went into their sitting room for tea, she would embroider in a new face. She said it wouldn't make any difference if the doll had awfully short arms and legs, if her face was pretty. She said, "And next summer we'll put corn silk hair on her and pin wild roses on her dress and she'll be just beautiful."

Eunice wiped her eyes on her sleeve and said, "I'm going to name her Nancy," and Plum said, "I think Marybelle Whistle would be more appropriate. Go on, Eunice, name her Marybelle and then I'll punch her in the stomach and hit her in the eye and stamp on her toes."

Eunice said, "No, I want her to be named Nancy. She's the only doll I've ever had."

Nancy said, "I have a good idea. I'll make a Marybelle Whistle doll. There are lots of rags and an old comforter in

34

the attic and I'll ask Mrs. Monday for a needle and some thread to do some mending."

The children wanted to know if she was going to make the doll that very evening and Nancy said that she might get started on her if she could sneak up to the attic. Speaking of the attic reminded Nancy and Plum of the trunk room and the empty box addressed to them and they pulled it out from under their bed and showed it to the other children, who all said that Marybelle had two very large new dolls. One with golden hair and one with black hair. Nancy and Plum asked how they were dressed and the children said that the blond one had on a pale blue velvet coat and bonnet trimmed with white fur and the dark-haired one had on a pale pink velvet coat and bonnet trimmed with brown fur. Eunice said that both dolls had on little white gloves and real little white galoshes. She also said that they were as large as real children and perfectly beautiful. As she told how beautiful Marybelle's new dolls were, she looked down at her own doll and began to cry again. "You're ugly, ugly, ugly," she sobbed, pounding on Quince Face's stuffed stomach with her fist. "Even with a new face you'll look like a tree with its branches sawed off. Here, Plum, make her into Marybelle Whistle, I never want to see her again."

She threw Quince Face at Plum, who grabbed her and put her in the big box under the bed, then stood up and announced, "Ladies and gentlemen: Tomorrow evening after supper I will present a play called 'REVENGE!' Admission is free, everybody is invited."

Eunice laughed then, and Nancy put her arm around her and said, "Perhaps I can make you a new doll out of the stuff in the attic. It may not be the prettiest doll in the world but it certainly won't be as ugly as Marybelle Whistle."

Then up the stairway and down the long corridor came the booming gong of the supper bell and the familiar smell of scorched oatmeal, and the children trooped down to supper.

Mrs. Monday and Marybelle were already seated at their special table, eating little hot chicken pies and baked apples and thick cream, and on each side of Marybelle, seated on little new red chairs, were two of the most beautiful dolls Nancy and Plum had ever seen. They were almost three feet tall, their thick shining real hair hung down their backs in long curls; their dresses were pale blue and pale pink silk; they each wore a white ruffled pinafore; their shoes were pale blue and pale pink Mary Janes and they each had dimples, real eyelashes and teeth.

"Oh, Marybelle," said Nancy, "what beautiful dolls. Did you get them both from your mother?"

Marybelle said, "No, stupid, my mother didn't give them to me. Aunty Marybelle did. Don't get so close to them, you might get them dirty."

Plum said, "It seems odd to me that you would get two dolls."

Mrs. Monday said, "Nancy and Plum, take your seats at the supper table and BE QUIET!"

It was Plum's turn to say the grace and when all the

children had bowed their heads Plum's clear sweet voice intoned with proper reverence but much louder than usual:

> "God is great and God is good,
> And we thank Him for this food.
> By His hand may we be led,
> Give us Lord our daily bread.
> And forgive us ALL FOR OUR SINS—
> *even stealing!*"

When Plum finished the grace she winked at Nancy, and Nancy, who had just taken a bite of oatmeal, choked. Plum didn't mind scorched oatmeal, in fact she thought scorching improved the flavor, but tonight, even though she was very hungry, it was so badly burned she couldn't eat it. Hungrily she turned and watched Mrs. Monday and Marybelle gorging themselves on their chicken pies until finally Marybelle looked up and caught Plum's watching eyes, whispered to Mrs. Monday, and Mrs. Monday said, "Pamela, either turn around and eat your supper or go to your room."

Plum said, "The oatmeal is so badly burned we can't eat it, Mrs. Monday. May I ask Katie for something else?"

Mrs. Monday said, "Katie has not returned from her Christmas holiday yet and there is nothing else."

Plum said, "Are there any more baked apples?"

Mrs. Monday said, "GO TO YOUR ROOM!"

But Plum didn't. She left the dining room and went up the

stairs, stamping loudly so that Mrs. Monday would be sure and hear her, then sneaked down the back stairs to the kitchen, slipped out the back door, went out to the barn where Old Tom was milking, told him about the burnt oatmeal and asked him if he'd get her a few apples from the root cellar.

Tom said, "Did you get the eggs I left for you this morning?"

Plum said, "Oh, yes, Tom, and they were perfectly delicious. Thank you very much."

Old Tom said, "Go get that dipper and bring it over here and I'll give you some of this nice warm milk. How old are you, Plum, about six?"

Plum said, "I'm eight years old and I'll be nine in June."

Old Tom said, "Well, you're sure little and scrawny for your age. You better eat more."

Plum said, "I eat everything Mrs. Monday gives me but she takes away my meals for punishment so much that I'm lucky if I get one meal a day."

Old Tom said, "Haven't you and Nancy got anyone—I mean, have you no relatives at all?"

Plum said, "We've only got Uncle John and he doesn't care a thing about us." Then Plum thought of the two dolls and so she said, "At least we didn't used to think he did."

"What changed you?" Old Tom said, remembering the two little girls spending Christmas Eve in the barn.

"Something we found in the trunk room this morning," Plum said. "Only please don't say anything. We're not sure yet."

"I won't say anything," Old Tom said. "Now come on and let's get some apples."

When Plum had her apron filled with big red apples, she tiptoed up to the back porch but Mrs. Monday was in the kitchen supervising the children while they cleared up and washed the dishes, and the front door was locked, so she went back to the barn and asked Old Tom if he would put the ladder up to the trunk room again. Old Tom agreed and so Plum skittered up the ladder, her teeth chattering and her hands like ice, opened the trunk-room window and wiggled through, and then Old Tom climbed up and handed her her apron full of apples.

She had just closed the window and was feeling her way in the dark around the trunks and boxes when she heard the flap, flap of Mrs. Monday's approaching feet. Quickly she crouched down behind a trunk as Mrs. Monday opened the door, held her lamp high and looked around. Seeing nothing but empty boxes and trunks, she turned and went out again shutting the door behind her. Plum waited until she heard Mrs. Monday's footsteps going down to the second floor, before she crept out of the trunk room, tiptoed down the stairs and peered down the long corridor to be sure all was clear. Then she ran as fast as she could down to her room but some instinct warned her to run softly and to stop outside her door and peer through the crack.

Sure enough, Mrs. Monday was sitting in the little chair by the window waiting for her. Quickly Plum ran next door into Eunice and Mary Burton's room, put the apron full of apples in their closet, tiptoed out into the hall again, ran all the way back to the stairway and then, with steps a little louder than normal, came sauntering back to her room.

When she came in Mrs. Monday said, "WHERE HAVE YOU BEEN?"

Plum said, "Out in the barn playing with the kittens," which was the truth.

Mrs. Monday said, "I told you to go to your room. You shall be punished."

Plum said, "Mrs. Monday, you are punishing me because you burned the oatmeal and it was so horrible I couldn't eat it."

Mrs. Monday said, "Pamela Remson, you are impudent and I will not tolerate impudence."

Plum said, "Mrs. Monday, you are a selfish greedy woman. You starve your boarders and you and Marybelle have delicious food. And even that wouldn't be so bad if we didn't have to watch you eat it. Why should you and Marybelle have chicken pies while we have to gag on burnt oatmeal?"

Mrs. Monday said, "You and Nancy are a bad influence on the other children. Tomorrow you will both spend the day in the attic."

Plum said, "Just a minute, Mrs. Monday. I want to show you something." She reached down and pulled the empty box from under her bed. Pointing to the address label, she said, "This box was sent to Nancy and me. What was in it and why didn't we get whatever it was?"

Mrs. Monday said, "Where did you get that box?"

Plum said, "We were locked out of the house and I had to climb in the window of the trunk room."

Mrs. Monday said, "I have nothing to conceal about that box, Pamela. It contained your bed linen for the year."

Plum said, "It looks to me like a box that dolls came in and I found hair stuck to the sides."

Mrs. Monday said, "Don't you dare accuse me of telling an untruth, Pamela Remson. You are getting completely out of hand and I shall have to take steps." Mrs. Monday's voice quivered with suppressed rage, her pale eyes stared just above Plum's shoulder and they were like ice.

"Get undressed and get into bed AT ONCE!" she said, picking up the box and stalking out of the room.

As soon as her footsteps could be heard going down the front stairs, Plum whisked into Mary and Eunice's room, got the apples and put them under her bed. Then when Nancy and the other children came upstairs after they had finished the dishes, she gave them each an apple and told them about Mrs. Monday.

Later on when she and Nancy were in bed eating their apples in the dark, Plum said, "You know, Nancy, I think Mrs. Monday was scared when I told her about the box. She was terribly angry and I know she'll punish me just steadily from now on, but I think she was scared."

Nancy said, "Well, I'm scared. Mrs. Monday is a very cruel woman and she's mean enough when she doesn't have a reason."

Plum said, "One good thing about all this is that I'm sure Old Tom is now our friend. He's never crabby any more and tonight he was so nice about getting the apples and helping me sneak back into the house."

Nancy said, "How were the kittens and St. Nick? Did they miss us?"

Plum said, "Oh, they were just darling! They've moved back into Buttercup's stall but they came running when I called them. I wonder if I couldn't sneak out and bring them up to the attic with us tomorrow. I'll bet Old Tom would put the ladder up for me."

Nancy said, "I asked Mrs. Monday for a needle and a spool of white thread and some scissors tonight and she gave them to me and tomorrow when we're in the attic I'm going to try and make a doll for poor little Eunice."

"That reminds me of something," Plum said, reaching under the bed and getting Marybelle Whistle, the rag doll. She threw her up in the air as hard as she could so that Marybelle thudded against the ceiling and then flopped back down on the floor.

"Oh, pardon me, dear Marybelle," Plum said in an exact imitation of Marybelle's high squeaky voice, "I didn't realize I had bumped into you. I hope I didn't hurt you."

Nancy said, "I can't help but feel sorry for that poor ugly old doll."

Plum said, "Tomorrow I'm going to ask Tom for some shavings and I'm going to really make her look like Marybelle. Doesn't it just make you sick to think of her having our two dolls?"

Nancy said, "Let's not think of it. Let's think about the dolls and the trunks of clothes they probably have and what's in the trunks."

Plum said, "You tell me what's in the trunks, Nancy. I'm not in a good pretending mood."

So Nancy began, "The trunks each have a tiny golden lock and a tiny golden key. When we put the keys in the locks and turn them, the locks snap open and then we lift the lids and the first thing that we see are little jewel cases. We open the jewel cases and inside are tiny strings of pearls, tiny gold rings, tiny little wrist watches, tiny gold lockets with our pictures in them, little gold and silver barrettes and lovely little strings of coral beads.

"After we have looked at all the jewels, we close the jewel boxes and open little oblong boxes. These are glove boxes and in them are little white kid gloves, tiny angora mittens, little blue kid gloves and tiny white string mitts. There are also little boxes filled with socks. All colors and all silk, boxes of hair ribbons, all colors, and boxes of belts and ties. Then we lift off the tray of our trunks and underneath we find stacks and stacks of pinafores, dresses, underwear, sweaters, skirts, coats, even little raincoats with galoshes and umbrellas. There are also beautiful costumes, skating costumes, skiing costumes, ballet dresses, angel costumes and fairy costumes. There are slippers and skates or skis for each costume, blue jeans, riding habits and little riding boots, all kinds of pretty school dresses and, I forgot, but in the top trays of the trunks there are boxes full of darling handkerchiefs to go in the pockets of the school dresses, and boxes filled with little purses to go with the different coats.

"There are also . . ." Nancy stopped to think of something else just wonderful that there could be in the doll trunks and while she was thinking she noticed that Plum had fallen asleep. Nancy turned over, put her arm under her pillow and watched the golden moonlight come sliding in over the window sill and flow across the floor. Eunice's doll lay in its path and as the clear cool light fell on her she looked so helpless and forlorn there on the cold floor that Nancy slipped out of bed, picked her up and took her back into bed with her.

After the icy floor, the bed seemed delightfully warm and cozy, and Nancy patted old Quince Face on her knobby head and crooned, "There, that's better, isn't it? Now you're warm and comfortable, you poor little ugly, unwanted doll."

Then Nancy fell asleep and Christmas Day was over.

4

Nanela

NANCY AND PLUM decided that the doll for Eunice must be quite large and very pretty so that, even though she was a rag doll, she wouldn't remind Eunice of old Quince Face. But Nancy found that making such a doll was easier said than done. In the first place all the sewing had to be done by hand and secretly without the knowledge of either Mrs. Monday or Marybelle. In the second place she had a terrible time with the stuffing and in the third place there wasn't anything in the attic that would do for hair.

For material Nancy used some empty flour sacks she found in a corner of the attic. After the sacks had been bleached and washed in the milk room by Old Tom, she and Plum, with the aid of a tin washbasin and one of Plum's old red hair ribbons, dyed them pink. At first the color was so bright that Plum said she was afraid the doll was going to look like a red-faced sneak with scarlet fever, but Nancy said she was sure a few more rinsings would turn the material a nice pale pink like doll skin, and it did.

While the material was in the attic drying, Nancy cut a pattern out of newspapers, using the picture of a little girl in a magazine for a model but making the legs and arms and body of the doll wider to allow for seams and stuffing. With a pattern, cutting out the doll was easy but the sewing, which had to be done with double thread, tiny stitches and often by moonlight, took a long, long time. At last, however, came the day when Nancy could start putting in the stuffing and the big pink thing on which she had been working so long would begin to look like a doll.

All the way home on the school bus, she and Plum and Eunice whispered about the doll and when they could work on it and how it was going to look. Marybelle, almost wild with curiosity, moved up next to Plum and said, "What are you planning?"

Plum said, "Oh, we're just talking about how much fun it will be when we get home. How dear, dear Mrs. Monday, your own Aunty Marybelle, will send us to our rooms to change from our old raggedy school clothes into our old raggedy play clothes. Then she'll send us to the cellar to carry up coal for her sitting-room fire, to the kitchen to peel vegetables for Katie, to the dining room to set the table, to the pantry to polish silver, out to the barnyard to gather the eggs and help feed the chickens, upstairs to dust the halls and clean the bathroom or to the washroom to iron. We have so much fun we can hardly wait to get home."

Marybelle said, "You're not telling the truth. That's not what you were talking about. I know it isn't, because you were smiling and looking happy."

Plum said, "Well, if you know what we were saying, why do you ask?"

Marybelle said, "If you don't tell me, I'll have your supper taken away."

Plum said, "It might have something to do with those two new dolls you got for Christmas."

Marybelle said, "Those two old things? What would you talk about them for?"

Plum said, "Oh, I have reasons. Something my Uncle John wrote to Nancy and me."

Marybelle said, "Your Uncle John never did write to you."

Plum said, "Didn't he?"

Marybelle said, "When did he write to you? What did he say?"

Plum said, "Curiosity killed the cat."

So Marybelle flounced up to Mr. Harris, the bus driver, and told him that Nancy and Plum and Eunice were being mean to her. Mr. Harris, who liked children and had been driving them to and from school for years and years, looked at Marybelle and said, "Well, that's a pleasant change. Now go back and sit down."

47

Marybelle said, "I'm going to tell Aunty Marybelle on you when I get home."

Mr. Harris said, "You just go right ahead. Tell her I called you a mean, ornery, nosy little troublemaker right in front of the whole school bus and maybe she'll wash out my mouth with soap."

All the other children laughed but Marybelle said, "Well, I'm going to tell on Nancy and Plum and Eunice as soon as I get home."

Mr. Harris said, "I don't doubt it at all and it won't be the first time."

Marybelle said, "You're mean and Nancy and Plum and Eunice are mean and I'm going to have their supper taken away."

Mr. Harris said, "Well, in that case I guess I better give them the doughnuts I had left over from lunch." He stopped the bus, opened his lunch box and gave Nancy and Plum and Eunice each a big sugary doughnut that his wife had made the night before.

Marybelle was so furious that her usually gray face turned as red as a tomato and the minute the bus stopped before the Boarding Home she jumped out and ran as fast as she could to tattle to Mrs. Monday.

As she got out, Mr. Harris said, "There goes the meanest young'un I've ever seen in all my life. I've been driving this school bus for fifteen years and I've never seen one to compare with her in just plain hatefulness."

Plum said, "You should live with her. She spies and tattles all day long."

Mr. Harris said, "Isn't it a pity that varmints like her always grow up strong and healthy."

Eunice said, "She should be healthy, she eats only delicatessens while we eat oatmeal and prunes."

"Zat so?" Mr. Harris said, hiding his smile. "Well, all these delicatessens haven't improved her looks any. She's not near as pretty as you prune and oatmeal eaters, if that's any consolation."

The children all laughed and trooped off the bus just as Mrs. Monday opened the front door and summoned Nancy, Plum and Eunice to her sitting room.

Eunice said, "Quick, what shall we tell her we've been whispering about?"

Plum said, "Tell her it's about valentines. Valentine's Day will be pretty soon."

Nancy said, "I'm not going to tell her anything. I'm going to tell her that Marybelle is a tattletale and that's why she can't be in on our secrets."

Plum said, "You'll only get in trouble."

Nancy said, "I don't care, we have a right to our own thoughts and plans. I won't lie."

Plum said, "I never feel that the things I tell Mrs. Monday are lies. I think that lies are only when you want not to tell the truth. With Mrs. Monday I want to tell the truth but life is easier if I don't."

Nancy said, "You're always braver than I am, Plum, but right now if Mrs. Monday burned me with red hot coals and beat me with a whip, I wouldn't tell her a lie and I would not tell her the truth."

Plum said, "All right. But remember we won't get any supper."

Eunice said, "I'll sneak some bread and butter for you."

Plum said, "You probably won't get any either."

Just then Marybelle came out smirking and said, "Aunty Marybelle says for you to come into her sitting room AT ONCE!"

Plum said, "All right, Sneaky Tattletale."

Marybelle said, "Aunty Marybelle told you never to call me Sneaky again, Plum Remson. I'm going to tell on you."

Plum said, "Go ahead and tell, Sneaky."

Marybelle stuck out her tongue at Plum and went back into the sitting room. The three little girls followed. Mrs. Monday was seated by the fire drinking tea and looking like a black vulture waiting for its prey. For a few minutes she stared at them but she did not speak. Then suddenly she lashed out, "Why do you whisper and torment poor little Marybelle? What are you planning?"

Nancy and Plum and Eunice said nothing.

Mrs. Monday said, "Answer me at once. What is all this talk about a letter from your Uncle John?"

No answer.

Mrs. Monday said, "If you do not answer me you will all stay in your rooms without supper."

The three children just stood there, so Mrs. Monday said, "Very well, go to your rooms, AT ONCE!" The "at once" was almost a shriek. Plum and Nancy and Eunice looked at each other and smiled.

When they got up to their room they changed from their school clothes and got to work on the doll. The stuffing out of the old comforter was in a sack in the back of their closet. Working as fast as they could with Plum guarding the door, Eunice and Nancy grabbed handfuls of the rather lumpy cotton and carefully poked it down into the legs and arms, the body and finally the neck and head of Little Nancy. When they had finished, Nancy stitched up the opening in the head and then held Little Nancy up for Plum to see.

Plum began to laugh. Nancy said, "What's the matter? Why are you laughing?"

Plum said, "She's so lumpy. She looks like she was born with long underwear on. We'll have to change her name to Squeaky Swanson."

Nancy said, "She is awfully lumpy, isn't she? It's that old wadded cotton."

Plum said, "If she wasn't so lumpy, she'd be perfect. She is a very nice shape and you've done a neat job of sewing her, Nancy."

Nancy said, "I wonder what else we could stuff her with?"

Plum said, "Straw. That's what they stuff scarecrows with. Remember when Miss Waverly read us the *Wizard of Oz?*"

Nancy said, "But straw's too stickery for a doll!"

Plum said, "Hay then. It's lots finer than straw. I'll climb out the window and shinny down the maple tree and tell Old Tom to get us some."

She did and came back in a few minutes with a gunny sack full of hay, which Nancy and Eunice stuffed inside of Little Nancy. When they finished the doll was as lumpy as ever but what was worse, fine pieces of the hay had poked through the cloth, making her look as though she had whiskers growing all over her.

Plum and Eunice laughed but Nancy was almost in tears until Plum had another idea. Sawdust. She said that she had read that in the olden days all the dolls were stuffed with sawdust. "Remember that poem, 'I once had a sweet little doll, dears, the prettiest doll in the world,' and remember how she left the doll out in the field and the cows ate her or something? Well, that doll was stuffed with sawdust."

Nancy said, "But where will we get the sawdust?"

Plum said, "From the woodshed. There's a big heap of it by the saw horse. It's kind of dirty and full of chips and sticks but Eunice and I can pick the rubbish out of it while you stuff Little Nancy."

So Nancy unstuffed Little Nancy and Plum took the sack of hay back down the tree. In a few minutes she came back with a bag partially filled with sawdust. As it was getting late and they were sure Mrs. Monday would be up right after supper to give them a lecture, to hurry things they dumped the sawdust in a heap on the floor and Plum and Eunice picked out the sticks and chips while Nancy rammed the stuffing into the doll.

When they were through, Little Nancy didn't have a

single lump and with the exception of her blank face and bald head looked almost like a little child.

Eunice said, "Of course, you made the doll, Nancy, but Plum was so wonderful about finding something to use for stuffing that I really think I should name her after Plum, too."

Plum said, "Well, if you name her after both of us you'll have to name her either Pancy or Numb." They all laughed.

Then Nancy said, "You could call her Nanela—that's a combination of Nancy and Pamela, and I think it's pretty."

"At least it's better than Pancy," Plum said.

So Nanela was named and hidden in the back of Nancy and Plum's closet while the three little girls tried to figure out what to do about her face and what to use for hair.

Nancy said that she could embroider a face if only she had some colored embroidery thread. She also said that she could make a beautiful wig out of yarn if only she had some yarn.

Plum said, "If Nanela is to be a combination of Nancy and me she will have to have striped hair. Red and yellow. Red for Nancy and yellow for me."

Nancy said, "No, she's not going to have striped hair. I'll make it yellow like yours, Plum."

Plum said, "I was really only fooling. I don't want Nanela to have striped hair. Why not make it brown like Eunice's?"

Eunice said, "I think Nanela's hair had better be any color yarn we can get."

A voice from the doorway said, "Why aren't you down helping Katie and what is the meaning of this mess?"

Nancy said, "You told us to stay in our rooms."

Mrs. Monday glared at the children, then at the hay, sawdust and little sticks that littered the floor. She said, "What on earth have you been doing? This place looks like a barn."

Plum said, "I was trying to make a bird's nest for natural history at school."

Mrs. Monday said, "Eunice, I told you to stay in your room. Why are you in here?"

Plum said quickly, "She has to make a bird's nest, too. We were working together."

Mrs. Monday said, "Well, pick up this mess at once. I'll be back later to talk to you."

When she had gone Nancy said, "Plum, you shouldn't tell things that aren't true. It's better to tell the truth and be punished than to tell a lie."

Plum said, "If we had told Mrs. Monday about Nanela she would have taken her and burned her and you know it."

Nancy said, "Yes, but what you said wasn't the truth at all."

Plum said, "I'll make it the truth then. I'll go down and get some more hay and I'll make Eunice and me each a bird's nest and we'll take them to school tomorrow and surprise Miss Waverly."

Nancy said, "Oh, Plum, that's a wonderful idea. Then you'll have told the truth and your heart won't turn black."

"What do you mean her heart won't turn black?" Eunice asked.

Nancy said, "Katie told us that every lie you tell makes a black spot on your heart."

"And," Plum said, "Nancy's afraid my heart's pitch-black already."

"Oh, no, I'm not," Nancy said, "but you're so much braver than I am and you talk to Mrs. Monday more than I do and she seems to make it necessary to tell lies."

Plum said, "Don't worry, Nancy, we're smarter than Mrs. Monday and Marybelle, and we can figure out a way to keep our hearts from getting all spotty."

Nancy said, "Well, the first thing we had better do is to clean up this room."

Plum said, "You start while I get the hay to make the bird's nests." Grabbing the sack, she opened the window and climbed out again.

Later, when Mrs. Monday made her promised visit, the room was clean, Nancy and Plum were in bed and on the study table by the window were two bird's nests made of thread and hay.

The next day when Eunice and Plum presented Miss Waverly with the nests she was pleased but quite surprised.

She said, "They're such nice nests that I think it would be a good idea for some of the boys to climb up and put them in that big apple tree outside the schoolroom window. Then if the birds do build in them we can watch them. If they don't use our nests, at least they'll be good examples of bird architecture. Did you make one, too, Nancy?"

Nancy said no and then because Miss Waverly was her favorite teacher and the person she liked best in all the world, she told her the whole story of Quince Face and Nanela.

When she was telling about Marybelle and Mrs. Monday, Nancy noticed that Miss Waverly's eyes blazed. When she told about Quince Face, Eunice's only Christmas present, Miss Waverly's eyes filled with tears. Nancy didn't mention the empty box and Marybelle's two new dolls or the fact that she and Plum had spent Christmas alone because those things didn't have anything to do with the bird's nests.

When she finished, Miss Waverly put her arm around her and said, "Would you like me to help you with Nanela?"

Nancy said, "Oh, yes, I've been so worried about getting the face right."

Miss Waverly said, "You bring Nanela to school tomorrow and I'll take her home with me and see if I can't give her a face and some hair."

Nancy said, "But how will I get her to school without Marybelle seeing her?"

Miss Waverly said, "I'll come down to the Boarding Home and get her, this very afternoon. I'll tell Mrs. Monday that you have been making something for me and then even if she does see the doll, it won't make any difference."

Nancy said, "Oh, thank you, Miss Waverly," and Plum and Eunice said, "Thank you, Miss Waverly," and then it was time to ring the bell.

True to her word, Miss Waverly picked up the doll that afternoon and took her home with her. Nancy and Plum and Eunice, with the impatience of children, were sure that she would be finished the next day or, at the very latest, in two days. But weeks went by and Miss Waverly not only didn't bring the doll but didn't mention it. Because Miss Waverly was their teacher and they were quite timid, Eunice and Nancy didn't dare ask her if she was working on the doll and when it would be finished.

Unfortunately, Plum, who would have been glad to ask Miss Waverly about Nanela, was so busy helping Old Tom build a calf pen for Buttercup's calf that was to be born on May Day, that she forgot all about Nanela. She didn't forget about Quince Face, however, and every day she saved the shaving curls from Tom's planing and every night pinned them on Quince Face and turned her into Marybelle Whistle, the main character in her continued play *Revenge*. During the course of the play, Marybelle was pinched, hit, tossed in the air, stamped on, run over, drowned, dropped off cliffs, scalped by Indians and dragged behind galloping horses until finally she lost one leg and one arm and it was impossible to tell her front from her back.

All the children loved Plum's play, especially as she always spoke so sweetly to Marybelle, begging her pardon very politely as she pushed her in front of a train or pointed out a beautiful flower growing right in the path of an avalanche.

One night when Marybelle was on the edge of a burning building (really Nancy and Plum's bureau) screaming for help and Plum as the Fire Chief with his siren going full blast was hurrying to the fire so that he could get Marybelle to jump off the one-hundred-story building into a net with a hole in it, Mrs. Monday came in and wanted to know what in the world was going on and what was all the noise. Plum said, truthfully, that she was giving a play.

Mrs. Monday said, "If you are giving a play, why wasn't Marybelle invited?"

Plum said, "But she was. She has the best part." And Mrs. Monday could not understand why all the children giggled.

That night Mrs. Monday ordered them all to bed but the next night she sent Marybelle up to join them and so Plum changed her play to a very dull lesson on how to build a calf pen. Fortunately Marybelle, who didn't care for animals, grew bored quickly, left and never returned, and Plum was able to continue with *Revenge* until Old Tom finally finished the calf pen and there were no more shaving curls.

By this time, Quince Face had been reduced to nothing but a dirty lump with no arms or legs. Nancy and Plum used her as a bean bag until the day that Mrs. Monday told Nancy and Plum they couldn't be in the Maypole dance at school and Plum, in a fit of anger, threw Quince Face out the window and over the high fence.

The very next day when the children got to school, Miss Waverly took them in the cloak room and handed Eunice her finished doll. They understood then why she had taken so long. Nanela was Beautiful. She had bangs and braids of soft brown yarn, a painted face with embroidered-on eyelashes and eyebrows that looked almost real, large blue eyes with a very merry expression, red smiling lips, a complete outfit of clothes, even to shoes and socks, a sweater which Miss Waverly had knitted, a white ruffled pinafore with a handkerchief in the pocket, a darling blue-and-white-checked school dress and white lacy underwear. Eunice was so excited she couldn't speak.

She just hugged Nanela, touched her pretty clothes and smiled at Miss Waverly.

Nancy said, "Miss Waverly, I think Nanela is the most beautiful doll in the world. Thank you for fixing her and making all those lovely clothes."

Miss Waverly said, "I haven't had so much fun in years, Nancy."

Nancy said, "Miss Waverly, just one thing. Will you please tell Mrs. Monday about Nanela so she and Marybelle won't try and take her away from Eunice."

Miss Waverly said, "I certainly will. This very afternoon," and she did.

Mrs. Monday said, "Of course, it was most kind of you to make the doll, Miss Waverly, but I'm afraid that you have wasted your time. Eunice is a very careless child and really cares nothing for dolls. Here is the proof."

She reached in a drawer in her desk and brought out the last remains of Quince Face, which Old Tom had found that morning and had given to Mrs. Monday thinking that perhaps it was the battered but favorite toy of one of the littler children. Mrs. Monday held Quince Face up in two disdainful fingers and said, "This is what is left of a lovely doll that one of Eunice's aunts made for her for Christmas. You can see the care it has had."

Miss Waverly took Quince Face, brushed her off, looked at the squinty, crooked face up high on the forehead and the thick, lumpy body and knew that this doll had never been anything but as ugly and unloveable as Nancy and Plum had described her. She said, "No doubt Eunice's aunt had the best intentions in the world when she made this doll, but though it certainly has had bad treatment, the original face is still here and it is hideous."

Mrs. Monday said, "I saw the doll when it was new and I thought it was charming."

Miss Waverly said, "I suppose that is a matter of taste. Anyway, I have made Nanela for Eunice and I wish her to keep her. If, in the past, she has been careless with her toys, perhaps having something that her teacher has made will make her more careful."

Mrs. Monday said, "I doubt it." But Miss Waverly knew that she wouldn't dare take Nanela away from Eunice.

5

The Sunday-School Picnic

EVERY SUNDAY MORNING at eight-fifty-five, Mrs. Monday's eighteen little boarders lined up in the front hall for inspection before Sunday School. Down the line went Mrs. Monday, checking ears, necks, fingernails, teeth and hair. She paid no attention to the clothes, which were all hand-me-downs and always either too large or too small, but she was most particular about straight parts, neat braids and polished shoes even when the shoes were so worn out that, as Plum said, "It was just like polishing your feet."

As the boarders passed inspection, and some of them were sent back upstairs as many as three or four times to wash necks, straighten parts or brush teeth, they were handed a penny for collection and sent out to the front gate to wait for Old Tom and the delivery truck.

None of the children looked forward to the ride to and from Sunday School for they had to ride in the back of the truck, which was dark and smelled of the feed and chickens Old Tom hauled in it. Not only that, but the seats along the sides were very hard and very narrow and when the truck went over bumps, which it did all the way to the church, the children either had to lean forward and take a chance of falling off the narrow seat or lean back and have their heads banged against the hard sides. Then, too, there was the usual amount of pinching and hair pulling, which, because of the darkness, always resulted in the wrong person being slapped.

Nancy and Plum hated the ride in the truck, with Marybelle in her pretty clothes riding in the front seat with Old Tom and the others crowded in the back and shaken around like popcorn in a popper. And they hated Miss Gronk, their Sunday-School teacher, who was old and parched, taught Sunday School because it was her duty and believed in long homework assignments in the way of memorizing verses from the Bible.

When they were reciting the Beatitudes, one of the children said:

"Blessed are the neat for they shall clear up the earth,"
instead of
"Blessed are the meek for they shall inherit the earth,"

and the other children laughed and Miss Gronk rapped with her pencil on the back of the pew and said, "Religiod is do laughig batter. Mariad bade an error and we should feel sorry for her. To bake sure there are do bore errors bade, I want you all to write the Beatitudes ted tibes ad brig theb to be next Sudday."

All winter long Miss Gronk had terrible head colds and called Nancy and Plum "Dadcy and Plub" and asked Marybelle how her dear aunt "Bisus Bodday was gettig alog."

Naturally Miss Gronk liked Marybelle and blamed all of Marybelle's wiggling and whispering on somebody else. Whenever Marybelle didn't know her Bible verses, which she never did, Miss Gronk would say, "Berrybell has bid sick, class, so the poor little thig could dot study." This of course made the members of the class who lived at Mrs. Monday's and knew that Marybelle had not been sick perfectly furious.

Once Plum said, "Miss Gronk, why do you always excuse Marybelle? She wasn't sick at all last week."

Miss Gronk said, "Pabbela Rebsod, I ab ruddig this Sudday-School class."

The other Sunday-School teachers were always having little parties for the children, picnics in the spring and summer, taffy pulls and skating parties in the winter, the accounts of which Nancy and Plum listened to with great longing.

"Out of all the teachers in that Sunday School why did we have to get that old 'Biss Grok,' " Plum said furiously one day as they were standing around waiting for church to begin and the other children were telling about a wonderful picnic their teacher had planned for them.

"I like Miss Gronk," Marybelle said, smoothing the fingers of her new white gloves.

Plum said, "Well, I hate her. She talks like she was stuffed with cotton, she smells like horse liniment and she acts like it was a sin to be alive.

" 'I'll dot tolerate smilig in by class, Pabbela,' she told me this morning. I said, 'I wasn't smiling. My lips just go that way,' and she said, 'Codtrol your lips, thed, Pabbela, we bust look dowdcast in the house of the Lord.' "

Mr. Conrad, the Sunday-School superintendent, who happened to overhear this conversation, had quite a time controlling his lips but he resolved to speak to Miss Gronk about her doleful attitude and the fact that she never had any little parties for her class.

So the next Sunday, Miss Gronk announced that on the following Saturday the class would have a picnic. "We will all beet at by house," she said. "You will each brig your owd lunch, we will go for a dice walk, eat the luch and returd hobe. Wear warb clothig and rebeber I will dot tolerate any wild akshuds such as racig or loud talk."

"Or smilig," Plum whispered to Nancy.

"Well, at least it's better than nothing," Nancy said to Plum as they were getting dressed Saturday morning.

"I'm not so sure," Plum said as she jerked the elastic off one of her braids. "She'll probably make us sit in a patch of nettles and write Bible verses."

Nancy said, "Oh, maybe we can get her to take us up to Lookout Hill. The kids at school say it's just beautiful up there. They say you can see for miles and miles and there are some tame squirrels that will eat out of your hand."

Plum said, "I suppose I should be glad because it's Saturday and we're getting away from Mrs. Monday and going on a picnic, but if only we weren't going with Miss Gronk!"

Nancy said, "Oh, come on, let's hurry with our work. It's a beautiful spring day and we can have a good time, in spite of Miss Gronk and Marybelle."

But when Old Tom let them off in front of Miss Gronk's little gray house, she thought she had never seen such a dreary looking place. All the blinds were drawn, there was a sign on the front steps "No solicitors" and a sign on the doorbell "Do not ring." Silently the children climbed the creaking steps to the front porch.

"Do you suppose she's home?" Eunice whispered to Nancy.

"It certainly doesn't look like it," Nancy said.

Marybelle said, "Oh, she's home. She always keeps her shades down. She says the sunshine fades her carpets." Boldly she strode up to the front door and knocked.

No one came. Marybelle knocked again, louder, and finally from the back of the house they heard shuffling feet and Miss Gronk opened the front door a crack and whispered hoarsely, "By cold's buch worse ad I shouldn't go but a probise is a probise. I'll be right out. Do doise dow—Baba's dot well." She shut the door.

Plum said, "I feel sad as though I was going to a funeral instead of a picnic."

Nancy said, "Well, anyway, it's a beautiful day. Let's start a dandelion chain."

Quickly the girls jumped off the porch and began picking

the fat, golden dandelions growing along Miss Gronk's fence. A robin watched them from a fence post until Miss Gronk's big white cat climbed up on another fence post to watch the robin.

Marybelle said, "Let's make a dandelion chain for Miss Gronk."

Plum said, "She won't like it."

Marybelle said, "Oh, she will, too. Miss Gronk's awfully sweet. I'm going to make her a dandelion necklace."

When Miss Gronk emerged from the house she was so bundled up, so wrapped in sweaters, scarves, coats and shawls that only her watery eyes were visible.

"Cob od, girls," she croaked, "pick up your luch bags and let's get started."

Marybelle ran up to her and said, "Bend down, Miss Gronk. I want to slip this beautiful dandelion chain around your neck."

Miss Gronk said, "Heaveds do, Barybelle, dadeliods give be hay fever." She turned to the other children who wore dandelion crowns, necklaces and bracelets. "I'll have to ask you to throw away all those dadeliods," she said. "I'b allergic to dadeliods."

Morosely the girls took off their crowns, bracelets and necklaces and threw them away.

"All right, lide up," Miss Gronk commanded. "Barybelle will walk with be. The rest of you stay in sigle file. Dow barch."

Like a funeral procession they started. First the old clothes bundle that was Miss Gronk, and Marybelle, then the ten little girls of the Sunday-School class, then Nipper, Miss Gronk's half-blind, very old dog.

The sky was a deep clear blue, the air was fragrant with apple blossoms and newly ploughed earth, birds chirped and trilled from every bush, chipmunks skittered around and around the tree trunks like stripes on a barber pole and the grass in the meadows billowed off into the distance in big soft rolling waves like the sea. It was a perfect day for a picnic. Plum wanted to run and sing and jump over a fence and climb a tree. Nancy wanted to lie on her back and look at the sky through the pink apple blossoms and listen to the birds. But Miss Gronk wanted to walk as slowly and as silently as a turtle and so that is what they did.

Plum said, "I hate Miss Gronk. She's spoiling the whole day."

Nancy said, "Let's pretend that underneath all those old coats and scarves and shawls is really a beautiful princess and if we believe in her and don't get angry with her, when we get to Lookout Hill she'll shed those old clothes and emerge all golden and beautiful."

Plum said, "All right, but how do you know we're going to Lookout Hill?"

Nancy said, "I just feel that we are and anyway the turnoff is ahead just a little way."

Plum said, "One thing I'm glad of. Old Marybelle's having a terrible time. I noticed that her eyes are already watering from the fumes of the horse liniment and she has to hold Miss Gronk's hand and you know how cold and damp Miss Gronk's hands always are."

Nancy said, "Oh, Plum, you shouldn't say anything about

the Princess. She is terribly sensitive about the ugly disguise she has to wear."

Plum said, "Nancy, look at the low branch on that big maple tree. I'm going to run over there, jump up and grab it and take one great big swing. I bet it'll be just like flying."

Nancy said, "Miss Gronk, I mean the Princess, won't like it."

Plum said, "I don't care. I just have to take one swing." And like a little fawn she jumped over the fence, ran across the field and leapt up and grabbed the branch. The branch bent down and she got a good hold, then lifted her feet off the ground and the branch swung up and then down, then up and down. Plum felt like a leaf in the wind, like a little beetle on a blade of grass, like a bee on an apple blossom. She forgot all about Miss Gronk, about everything but the fact that it was spring and she was a little girl swinging in a tree.

Then she heard Nancy calling, "Plum, come on. Miss Gronk will be mad as anything."

Plum took one last big swing that lifted her way up into the branches of the tree and then let go. Her hands were red and burning from holding on to the bark but she felt wonderful, alive and happy and wonderful.

She called to Nancy, who was coming across the field toward her, "Come on, Nancy, take one swing. It's like magic."

Nancy said, "Well, maybe just one. We can catch up to Miss Gronk in a second, she walks so slow."

She jumped and grabbed the branch and swung up, up, up into the tree, then way down to the ground, where Plum was waiting, her blue eyes bright with happiness. Nancy, too, felt like a leaf, a bee on a flower and a flower in the wind. Again and again she swung and then Plum took a turn, then Nancy another turn and another and the time flew by and pretty soon they stopped to rest and realized that it was almost noon and Miss Gronk and the picnic were nowhere in sight.

Grabbing their lunch bags, they jumped over the fence and ran down the road clear to the turnoff for Lookout Hill before they saw Miss Gronk and the Sunday-School class far ahead of them.

"Oh, Nancy," Plum wailed, "she isn't going to Lookout Hill at all."

Nancy said, "I wonder if she saw the sign."

Plum said, "Of course she saw it. It's about ten feet high. Where do you suppose she is going?"

Nancy said, "I know. She's going to the cemetery. See, she's taking the hill past the church."

Plum said, "Well, I'm not going to a picnic in the cemetery. I'm going up Lookout Hill."

Nancy said, "Do we dare?"

Plum said, "Yes, we dare. Here we go," and she waved good-bye to Miss Gronk and the Sunday School and turned up the hill.

The path to Lookout Hill was long and very steep but it led through the woods and the trees were shady and the pine needles were springy and there were bluebells in the crevices of the rocks. Nancy and Plum grew very tired and very hungry but they had made up their minds not to stop nor to eat their lunch until they reached the Lookout place. And they didn't.

About three o'clock Nancy said, "I wonder if we're on the right path. We've been climbing for hours and we should be there now."

Plum said, "The sign said Lookout Hill and it pointed this way. Come on, I'll race you around the next curve."

Nancy said, "You go on. I'm too tired." Plum ran around the curve and came back calling, "We're there! We're there! Hurry up, you can see for a thousand miles!"

Nancy grabbed Plum's hand and together they ran around the last curve and then they were leaning against the old stone wall that marked Lookout Hill. Far, far down below them, a river was trying to wriggle its way out of a steep canyon. Over to the right, thick green hills crowded close to each other to share one filmy white cloud. To the left, as far as they could see, the land flowed into valleys that shaded from a pale watery green, through lime, emerald, jade, leaf, forest, to a dark, dark bluish-green, almost black. The rivers were like inky lines, the ponds like ink blots.

Nancy said, "I feel just like an angel flying around and looking down at the earth."

Plum said, "Let's live up here. Let's pitch a tent right here and live on nuts and berries like pioneers."

Nancy said, "Let's eat our lunch right now. I'm starving."

Plum said, "Look, hard-boiled eggs, peanut-butter sand-wiches and apples. Katie must have fixed the lunches."

Nancy said, "Oh, Plum, see! A little squirrel. Look, there below the wall. Here, little squirrel, here's a tiny peanut-butter sandwich." Nancy broke off a piece of her sandwich and tossed it down to the squirrel. He picked it up in his paws, stuffed it in his mouth and ran off.

Plum said, "I wonder if Miss Gronk has started home yet."

Nancy said, "I wouldn't doubt it. She probably made the children line up on tombstones, choke down their lunch and then start right back. I wonder what she brought in her lunch. It was an awfully big bag."

Plum said, "The bag was probably filled with medicines. I'm glad we don't have to watch old Marybelle eating her special lunch with fried chicken and little cupcakes. I hope Miss Gronk's liniment smelled so awful it made Marybelle sick. Say, I bet if we ran all the way down from here we can be at the path before they get there."

Nancy said, "We'd better, otherwise Miss Gronk will go right over and tell Mrs. Monday."

Plum said, "Let's feed the squirrels a few more sandwiches, fill our eyes with the view so we can never forget it and then run."

Nancy said, "The way to remember how it looks up here is to look, then close your eyes and see if you can still see it. If you can't, then keep looking until you can."

Side by side they stood by the stone parapet, staring at the view, closing their eyes tight, then staring again. When at last they thought they could remember everything, they turned and started down the path. Going down was so easy they fairly flew. Sometimes they ran, sometimes they took big jumps and slid on the slick pine needles and sometimes in the steepest places they sat down and slid. When they got to the turnoff they were quite breathless. They decided to rest before starting for Miss Gronk's house.

Plum lay on her back, arms folded under her head, looking up into a tall pine tree. She said, "I think I'll be a tramp when I grow up. I love to be outdoors and tramps have a lot of fun."

Nancy said, "I'm going to get married and have twelve children and every single day in the week I'll give them a party, or a taffy pull, or a real picnic, or a . . ."

Plum said, "Hush, be quiet a minute. I think I hear Miss Gronk and the children. Let's pretend that we've been waiting here for them." .

Nancy said, "We'll pretend we couldn't find them."

Plum said, "I've got a better idea. Let's hide behind the sign until they get past, then tag along at the end of the line as though we had been there all the time. I'll bet old Miss Gronk won't even know."

"I'll bet Marybelle will though," Nancy said.

Plum said, "Let's try it anyway."

So when Miss Gronk and the sad little Sunday Schoolers filed past, Nancy and Plum waited a minute, then got into line behind Nipper.

Eunice, who was the last in line, said, "Where were you kids, I waited and waited for you."

Plum said, "Don't tell anybody but we went up to Lookout Hill."

Eunice said, "It was awful in the cemetery. Miss Gronk drank soup out of her thermos bottle and then took a nap. I wandered around reading the tombstones and smelling the flowers but it was awfully dreary. The other kids started a game of hide and seek but Miss Gronk said it wasn't respectful to the dead. What is it like at Lookout?"

Nancy and Plum told her and Eunice said that it sounded just like the time she rode in the Ferris wheel and could see for miles and miles. She said that Miss Waverly had told her that they might go up to Lookout on the school picnic.

Plum said, "Did Miss Gronk say anything about our not being with you at the cemetery?"

Eunice said, "No, she didn't even notice. She was too busy taking pills and rubbing liniment on her throat. Marybelle asked me where you were and I said you were at the other end of the cemetery playing house. She acted as if she didn't believe me."

Nancy said, "I'm sorry you didn't get to go with us, Eunice, but we didn't even know we were going ourselves. We stopped to swing in a tree and you all got ahead of us and then we saw the Lookout sign."

Plum said, "Come on, there's the tree. Let's have one swing before we go home."

Nancy said, "We'd better not, Plum. Marybelle will tell and then maybe we can't go to the school picnic."

Plum said, "Oh, all right."

Miss Gronk said, "Hurry up, girls. Old Tob is waitig ad I dough you're all tired frob your busy day."

Plum and Nancy said, "Thank you for the nice time, Miss Gronk, and we hope your cold is much better."

Miss Gronk said, "Hurry up, girls, dod't keep Tob waitig."

When they got home, Mrs. Monday shooed them into the kitchen and said, "Well, you've certainly had a nice day and I hope I won't hear another word about picnics for a long time."

Marybelle said, "Oh, Aunty Marybelle, we had a horrid time. Miss Gronk smells awful and we ate in the cemetery."

Mrs. Monday said, "In the cemetery? Why in the world did she go there?"

Marybelle said, "She had a terrible cold and anyway she wanted to put flowers on her sister Lulu's grave. She wouldn't let us talk. She made us walk single file and she spilled liniment on me and in my lunch basket."

Mrs. Monday said, "It certainly doesn't sound like much of a picnic. Were the other children nice to you?"

Marybelle said, "Nancy and Plum sneaked off and hid from me."

Mrs. Monday said, "Why did you hide from Marybelle, Nancy and Pamela?"

Plum said, "We weren't hiding from her. We were hiding from Miss Gronk. Her liniment smells awful and her hands are cold and damp."

Marybelle said, "And she made me hold her hand all day."

Mrs. Monday said, "Well, at least you got out in the fresh air, now let's hear no more about it. Nancy and Pamela, if I am not mistaken, it is your turn to set the table. Go and wash your hands and get to work."

That night after they were in bed, Nancy said, "You know,

Plum, I can close my eyes and it's just as if I was back on Lookout Hill, I can see everything so plainly."

Plum said, "I can close my eyes and remember exactly how it felt to be swinging in that tree."

Nancy said, "Poor old Miss Gronk, with nothing in her head but colds and sad thoughts."

6

A Magic Carpet

IT WAS A CLEAR WARM SATURDAY AFTERNOON, late in May. Miss Appleby, the Heavenly Valley librarian, and about twenty-eight children, ranging in age from five to thirteen years, were holding a story-telling session on the lawn in front of the little library building.

In the process of getting settled, there had been the usual amount of high-spirited roggling, wrestling and jostling for positions close to Miss Appleby, but the minute her warm, pleasant voice began "And the secret garden bloomed and bloomed and every morning revealed new miracles . . ." the children had become as motionless and quiet as the grass on which they sprawled. Now the only sounds that competed with Miss Appleby's reading were necessary sniffs or loud swallows and the buzz of an occasional inquisitive bee.

Miss Appleby, her library books and her story-telling sessions were very popular with all the children in Heavenly Valley. To Nancy and Plum they were a magic carpet that whisked them out of the dreariness and drudgery of their lives at Mrs. Monday's and transported them to palaces in India, canals in Holland, pioneer stockades during Indian wars, cattle ranches in the West, mountains in Switzerland, pagodas in China, igloos in Alaska, jungles in Africa, castles in England, slums in London, gardens in Japan or, most important of all, into happy homes where there were mothers and fathers and no Mrs. Mondays or Marybelles.

Of course, as soon as Mrs. Monday realized how important reading and Library Day were to Nancy and Plum, she either gave them so many extra chores to do that they had to get up at dawn in order to finish in time for Old Tom to drive them to town or she kept them at home as a punishment for some slight little mistake, usually something Marybelle had made up. Unfortunately for her, one spring, in a fit of spite, she kept them at home for three times in succession and Miss Appleby, having learned from the other children the reason for Nancy and Plum's absences, took the matter up with their teacher. The result was a letter to Mrs. Monday from the principal of the school, stating that he considered Library Day a most important part of education and from then would excuse only children too sick to walk.

Mrs. Monday, who didn't believe in libraries or reading but

didn't want an investigation of her methods of punishment, replied that from then on Nancy and Plum could attend Library Day but she would not be responsible for any book fines. The principal showed Mrs. Monday's letter to Miss Appleby, who said that if necessary she would pay the fines herself. She said, "My story-telling sessions and reading the books they borrow from the library are obviously the only pleasures those poor little mites have. What kind of a woman is this Mrs. Monday anyway?"

Miss Waverly, who had come to the library with the principal, said, "Well, all I know is that she is tall and gaunt, doesn't smile with her eyes and is very strong on punishment. I sometimes wonder if those children have enough to eat. They are all so small and scraggly looking."

Miss Appleby said, "Do Nancy and Plum have any parents?"

Miss Waverly said, "No they have not. They have been at Mrs. Monday's year in and year out for a long time."

Miss Appleby said, "What is the matter with people who dump children in boarding homes without investigating them first. Of course, Mrs. Monday's children are all very well behaved, use correct English and have nice manners but, with the exception of Nancy and Plum, they are all so subdued, so sad and so timid."

Miss Waverly said, "I believe that you are responsible for Nancy and Plum's fine spirit."

"What do you mean?" Miss Appleby asked.

"I mean," Miss Waverly said, "that you have encouraged

them to read, which has given them wisdom and understanding and humor way beyond their years."

Miss Appleby said, "Well, I wish I had enough money to give them a big meal with every story-telling hour."

Miss Waverly said, "Sometimes food for the soul is more important than food for the body. I wish I could learn more about Nancy and Plum. They don't seem to know anything about their background beyond the fact that their parents were killed in a train wreck and they are supposed to be in the care of an uncle who has never written or been to see them since he deposited them in Mrs. Monday's Boarding Home."

Miss Appleby said, "I'd like to have a chance to talk to that uncle or any of the other people responsible for those little waifs that live with Mrs. Monday."

Miss Waverly said, "Just wait until I tell you about Christmas and the doll Eunice's aunt gave her."

When she got through with the story, Miss Appleby said, "Where did Nancy and Plum go for Christmas?"

Miss Waverly said she didn't know. She hadn't asked them. She said, "Nancy and Plum are proud. They don't complain. The only reason I learned anything at all about Christmas was because they needed help in making that doll for Eunice."

Miss Appleby said, "The thing that makes me so boiling mad is that I know of at least a dozen homes right here in Heavenly Valley where a child would be as welcome as sunshine. Homes where they either don't have children or their children are grown up."

Miss Waverly said, "Oh, I know but what are you going to

do? Mrs. Monday won't give out any information and you can't take the children away from her without their parents' or guardians' consent. All we can do is to make the little time they spend with us as happy as possible. My only trouble is that every single time I plan a picnic or a play or anything that is going to be fun, Mrs. Monday manages to keep the children home. All except Marybelle, of course, she has and does everything."

Miss Appleby said, "She is the only child I ever have any trouble with here in the library. Speaking of trouble, it's almost time for the children, so I'd better get busy."

So, here they were out on the lawn and Miss Appleby was just finishing *The Secret Garden*.

" 'Across the lawn came the Master of Misselthwaite and he looked as many of them had never seen him. And by his side with his head up in the air and his eyes full of laughter walked as strongly and steadily as any boy in Yorkshire—Master Colin!'

"And that," said Miss Appleby, "is the end of *The Secret Garden*."

"May I take it home and read it over again?" asked Nancy.

"But, Nancy," Miss Appleby said, "you've read *The Secret Garden* four times already."

Nancy said, "I don't care. When I read it I forget I live at Mrs. Monday's and I run on the moors with Dickon and I go through those hundred rooms with Mary and I look at books with Colin."

Miss Appleby said, "That's the wonderful thing about

reading. You can go anywhere in the world, you can live a hundred, even a thousand different lives, you can learn about everything."

Plum said, "To be a librarian do you have to read every book there is?"

Miss Appleby said, "Goodness no. But I have read a great many. Probably more than a thousand."

Plum said, "How many books had you read when you were almost nine, like me?"

Miss Appleby said, "Well, when I was nine years old I lived with my grandmother and grandfather, who were very, very strict, very, very industrious people who didn't believe in wasting a single minute. Unfortunately they considered reading wasting time, and so I had to do all my reading secretly. I went to a little country school and the teacher, who was very understanding, used to keep me after school supposedly to clean the blackboards, but in reality so that I could curl up by the stove and read. She loaned me all of her books and I read *Black Beauty*, *The Adventures of Robin Hood*, *Treasure Island*, *Heidi*, *Rebecca of Sunnybrook Farm*, *Anne of Green Gables*, *Hans Brinker and the Silver Skates*, *The Jungle Book*, *The Water Babies*, *Timothy's Quest*, *Tom Sawyer* and *Huckleberry Finn*, *Dandelion Cottage*, *The Live Dolls*, *Sara Crewe*, *Little Lord Fauntleroy*, *Toby Tyler*, *The Secret Garden*, *Pinocchio*, *Robinson Crusoe*, *King Arthur*, *David Copperfield*, *Oliver Twist* and, of course, all of the fairy tales."

Nancy said, "Did your grandfather find out?"

Miss Appleby said, "Yes he did. One day a blizzard was blowing up and he came to school to get me and found me curled up in a chair by the stove reading *Sara Crewe*. He said, 'Evangeline Appleby, you are a wicked little girl and you have deliberately deceived me. You led your grandmother and me to believe that you had to stay after school to help the teacher and now I find you wasting your time reading. I am going to give you a whipping when you get home.'

"Ordinarily I was scared to death of my grandfather, who was a tall, stern old man. But this day I had just gotten to the part in *Sara Crewe* after Sara's father dies, when Miss Minchin is being horrible to Sara and Sara is up in the attic hungry and cold, talking to her doll Emily and she says, 'When people are insulting you, there is nothing so good for them as not to say a word—just to look at them and *think* . . . there's nothing so strong as rage, except what makes you hold it in, that's stronger.' I knew that my grandfather was very, very angry because his voice shook when he spoke to me, his face was mottled, blue veins stood out on his temples and his blue eyes had turned almost black. But I stood up and faced him and I wasn't Evangeline Appleby, the fat little girl who shivered and got tears in her eyes every time her grandfather spoke to her, I was Sara Crewe facing Miss Minchin and I was brave and strong. I said, 'Grandfather, reading is not wasting time. Reading is learning and you may whip me if you like but I am going to read every chance I get.'

"Well, my grandfather looked very surprised. He said, 'Have

you been reading here all winter?' and I said, 'I certainly have. I have read about twenty books.' My grandfather just said, 'Twenty books?' and I said, 'Maybe more.' He said, 'Twenty books is an awful lot of reading for one little girl.'

"My teacher, who had been sitting quietly at her desk correcting some papers, spoke up then and said, 'Twenty books is a lot of reading and a lot of learning, Mr. Appleby, and that is why we are skipping Evangeline to the fifth grade.'

"When we got in the sleigh to go home, the wind was whining and it was snowing awfully hard and Grandfather told me to keep the robe tucked tight around me. That's all he said. Not a word about the reading or skipping to the fifth grade. Old Charlie, the horse, seemed in a hurry to get home and we flew along, the snow stinging our faces, the wind screaming and jerking at the robe. Darkness was creeping in over the mountains and the road got harder and harder to make out. Once we went over a big bump and Grandfather said, 'That was a fallen log. We must be off the road.' He stopped the horse and got out of the sleigh and felt around in the snow with his hands. When he got back in he said, 'We may be lost. I can't make out a thing in this storm.'

"I said, 'What do you think we had better do, Grandfather?' and he said, 'Just keep on driving. That's all we can do. If we stand still we'll freeze to death.' His voice was thin and worried, so I said, 'Would you like me to tell you a story, Grandfather? The story of one of those books I've been reading?'

"He said, 'Well, it might help to keep us awake.'

"So I told him the story of King Arthur and the Round Table. I chose that one because it was history and I thought he might approve of history and anyway I had read it just before *Sara Crewe* and could remember it very well. I told about the knights and the jousting and the wicked Sir Mordred and Lancelot and The Holy Grail and Elaine and Guinevere and I grew so interested I forgot all about the snowstorm and the rough, raw wind and my feet like lumps of ice under the robe. I guess Grandfather got very interested, too, because I noticed that he let the reins go slack while he asked me questions about the drawbridges and the castles and the knights' armor.

"Then suddenly our horse stopped. 'Giddayup,' Grandfather shouted above the wind, but the horse wouldn't move.

"I was scared. 'Oh, Grandfather,' I wailed. 'Charlie is standing still and we'll freeze to death.'

" 'Giddayup, you old fool!' Grandfather yelled again, slapping Charlie hard with the reins. But Charlie just stood there.

"Grandfather jumped out of the sleigh, put his hand on Charlie's flanks to guide himself, so he could walk ahead to try and find out why Charlie was balking. He was bending over, rummaging around in the snow up by Charlie's head, when suddenly a lantern appeared out of the darkness and Grandmother's voice said, 'What in the world's the matter, Hector?'

"Grandfather straightened up and he felt pretty foolish. You see, Charlie the horse had brought us home. Charlie really saved our lives but Grandfather gave all the credit to the story of King Arthur I had told him. He said that if I

85

hadn't gotten him so interested in the Knights of the Round Table he would never have let the reins go slack and given old Charlie his head and we might still be out in that blizzard. From that day on as long as I lived with them, he and Grandmother drove me to the library every single Saturday and for every Christmas and birthday they gave me a new book."

Plum said quietly to Nancy, "I wish I could get Mrs. Monday out in a sleigh in a blizzard. I wouldn't tell her a story, I'd push her out of the sleigh."

Nancy said, "That was a wonderful story, Miss Appleby. You know, I used to read books and then tell the stories to the children during darning and sock-mending time and it made the work go so much faster and the children just loved it."

Miss Appleby said, "Do you still tell them stories, Nancy?"

Nancy said, "No, Mrs. Monday said that telling stories slowed up my mending too much."

Plum said, "Every single time I get to an interesting part in a book, Mrs. Monday says, 'Satan finds some mischief still for idle hands to do' and makes me hem napkins."

Miss Appleby said, "Perhaps I should call on Mrs. Monday and see if I can interest her in reading. Maybe I should invite her to these story-telling sessions."

Plum said, "Oh, don't, please don't. She'd make us all sit bolt upright with our hands folded in our laps and every time you'd get to a terribly exciting part she'd interrupt and say, 'Pamela, time to bring up the coal for my sitting-room fire . . .' or, 'Nancy, start polishing the brass immediately.'"

Plum's imitation of Mrs. Monday was so perfect that Miss

Appleby laughed, but Marybelle said, "I'm going to tell on you, Plum Remson. I'm going to tell Aunty Marybelle that you mocked her."

Miss Appleby said, "Plum didn't mean any harm, Marybelle. She was just explaining that Mrs. Monday might be bored by our reading aloud."

Marybelle said, "She mocked her. I heard her."

Miss Appleby said quickly, "What is your favorite book, Marybelle?"

Marybelle said, "Oh, any one with a lot of pictures. I don't like to read, I just like to look at the pictures."

Plum said, "If you'd look in a mirror you'd see the funniest picture of all."

Miss Appleby said, "Come, come, girls. Hurry and choose your books or I'll be driving home in the dark just like Grandfather."

Because Nancy and Plum were intelligent, imaginative children and because she had a fair idea of the atmosphere in the Boarding Home, Miss Appleby always recommended to them the stories that she had loved when she was a child on her grandfather's farm. She knew that after reading *Oliver Twist*, *David Copperfield*, *Nicholas Nickleby*, *Rebecca of Sunnybrook Farm* or *Anne of Green Gables*, Nancy and Plum would find their lot at Mrs. Monday's not quite so hard.

Miss Appleby loved Nancy's dreamy gentleness and recognized it by giving her special little girl books such as *Dandelion Cottage* and *The Live Dolls*. She also admired Plum's daring and quick humor and always saved her books about pioneer children who fought Indians or little Rebels who were spies in the Civil War.

Next to Miss Waverly, the children loved Miss Appleby more than anyone in the whole world and Nancy decided that when she grew up she was going to be a librarian.

She said, "Imagine sitting all day long in a room filled with hundreds and hundreds of books."

Plum said, "And all the fine-money for your very own. I'd fine everybody and I'd buy a great big bag of candy every day."

Miss Appleby said, "But the fine-money doesn't belong to the librarian, Plum, it belongs to the library and is used to help keep up the books. A fine is just a little reminder not to be selfish. That somebody else would like to read the book you have."

Plum said, "If I was a librarian and Mrs. Monday came in to get a book, I'd say, 'I'm sorry, Madam, but the only book we have left is this great big huge dictionary,' and then I'd drop it on her toes."

Miss Appleby said, "I really think that Nancy would make the best librarian, Plum, why don't you be a cowgirl?"

Plum said, "That's just what I was going to be. I'll ride my horse up to Nancy's library and lasso the books right off the shelves."

Miss Appleby laughed and said, "Well, whatever you and Nancy decide to be when you grow up, I know that you'll be happy because you have discovered the comfort and joy of reading."

7

A Letter to Uncle John

As THE MORNING BELL SOUNDED its harsh *clang! clang! clang!* Plum jumped out of bed and ran to the window to see what kind of a day it was. Pushing aside a branch of the maple, whose limp, shining leaves looked as if they had been cut out of green oilcloth, she saw that the valley was wrapped in a mist as thick and white as a caterpillar's cocoon. A mist that hid all of the barn but its roof, all of the orchard but a few upper branches, and made the familiar early morning sounds of chuffing mail train, mooing cows, cackling hens, peeping birds and crowing roosters, muffled and choky like Miss Gronk clearing her throat.

Plum looked all around, breathed in deep breaths of the cool, damp air and waited for the sun. When it came up finally, round and orange and thinly coated with white, Plum thought it looked like a giant poached egg but she knew it would clear the mist and make another beautiful day.

She turned and called to Nancy, "Hey, Nancy, get up. The sun's up and it's going to be a beauty day."

Nancy rolled over, burrowed her head in the pillow and said nothing.

Plum said, "Oh, look, here's our robin to say good morning. Good morning, Robbie Robin. My, you're getting fat. Mrs. Monday's bread pudding must agree with you."

Turning again toward Nancy, Plum said, "Today's the first of June. It's summer and next Friday's the program and the school picnic. Come on, Nancy, get up. It's our turn to set the breakfast table and we'd better be prompt or Mrs. Monday will keep us home from the picnic."

Nancy said, "I don't want to get up. I never want to get up again."

Plum said, "What's the matter. Are you sick?"

Nancy said, "No, I'm not sick but I hate everything." Her voice was muffled by the pillow but she sounded as if she might be crying.

Plum peered at her anxiously. "Nancy," she said, "are you sure you aren't sick?"

Nancy lifted her head and she was crying. She said, "Oh, Plum, what will I do? Miss Waverly wants me to sing a solo on the program for the last day of school and I can't get up before the whole school in my fadey short old school dress and my worn-out shoes. I'll look just hideous. All long, thin legs, like a stork with red hair."

Plum said, "Maybe you could borrow one of Eunice's dresses."

Nancy said, "Her clothes are as bad as mine and anyway I'm taller than she is now."

Plum said, "My clothes are awfully short too and my shoes have such big holes I'm afraid my feet will wear out but of course I'm only going to be in that old spelling match."

Nancy said, "I'll just die if I have to stand on the platform in that awful blue middy dress. It's been two years since I had a new school dress and even then it wasn't new, it was a hand-me-down of Marybelle's."

Plum said, "I know, I'll write to Uncle John."

Nancy said, "What good will that do? He never answered any of our other letters."

Plum said, "Maybe he never got 'em. Maybe Mrs. Monday never mailed them."

Nancy said, "Well, how can you be sure he'll get this one?"

Plum said, "You write the letter. Tell Uncle John about school and how you have to have a new dress and right after breakfast I'll sneak out and mail it."

Nancy said, "How will you get out? It's Saturday and you know Mrs. Monday keeps all the gates locked and you can't climb over that spiked fence. I wish it was Library Day."

Plum said, "I'll go under the fence."

Nancy said, "Jimmy tried to dig a hole under the fence and he said it is all cement."

Plum said, "I wish I had some firecrackers, I'd take out all the powder and blast my way out."

Nancy said, "Have you ever looked to see if the fence is broken any place?"

Plum said, "I haven't but the other kids have, lots of times."

Nancy said, "Uncle John must be paying for us or Mrs. Monday wouldn't keep us here. Maybe Uncle does send us clothes and Mrs. Monday never gives them to us."

Plum said, "You'd better get up or we'll be late setting the table and you know how anxious Mrs. Monday is to find an excuse to keep us home from the picnic."

Nancy said, "If you'll set my share of the table I'll stay up here and write the letter."

Plum said, "All right, but you better hurry. We have to braid our hair, remember."

Nancy ran into the bathroom and splashed cold water on her face and jerked on her play clothes. She and Plum combed and braided each other's hair and then Plum ran downstairs to set the table.

Nancy sat down at their study table, got out her school tablet, found a clean page, wet her pencil with her tongue so that the writing would be nice and black like ink and began:

Dear Uncle John:

Plum and I are very well and we hope you are too. We don't like to bother you but we are going to be in a

program at school, I am going to sing a solo and Plum
is going to be in a spelling match—she is the best
speller in school although only in the fifth grade—and
our school clothes are all worn out and much too short
and we wonder if you would ask Mrs. Monday to buy us
something new to wear. Just nice school dresses and new
shoes. Remember I have red hair and can't wear pink and
Plum looks terrible in green. Please have Mrs. Monday
get the dresses long enough and we would both like full
skirts. I have written to you several times but I guess you
have been too busy to answer.

Your loving niece,
Nancy Remson

Nancy addressed the letter to Mr. John Remson, Croquet
Club, Central City, and put it down inside her blouse. She
was in her place at the dining-room table before Mrs. Monday
and Marybelle emerged from their suite.

As they bowed their heads for grace, Nancy showed Plum
a corner of the letter. While they were eating their oatmeal,
she asked, "Do you have any good ideas?"

Plum said, "Yes, I'm going to tie the letter around a big
rock and I'm going to stand by the gate and throw it into a car
that is driving past."

Nancy said, "Oh, that's a wonderful idea. The rock will
break the windshield and hit the driver in the head and he'll
run off the road and bang into the fence and we'll escape
through the hole in the fence."

They both laughed and Plum was glad because she knew then that Nancy felt better.

Nancy said, "You could give the letter to Old Tom to mail."

Plum said, "I wouldn't dare. He's our friend and he is nice to us but he's afraid of Mrs. Monday and he does just what she tells him to. I wish we had a pigeon."

"What for?" Nancy asked.

"To be a carrier pigeon," Plum said. "You know how they send messages tied to pigeons' legs."

"Well, we don't have a pigeon," Nancy said, "so we'll have to think of some other plan. Oh, we just have to mail that letter, Plum. We can't go to the school program looking like scarecrows."

Plum said, "I have to help Tom clean out the chicken house this morning, but you give me the letter and maybe I'll think of something."

After breakfast, Nancy was just about to hand Plum the letter when Marybelle came sauntering up.

She said, "What are you two whispering about?"

Plum said, "We were talking about the program next Friday. Nancy's going to sing a solo."

Marybelle said, "I'm going to recite *Hiawatha*."

Plum said, "What, *all* of it?"

Nancy said, "Aren't you scared?"

Marybelle said, "Heavens, no! I've taken elocution lessons for years and years. Are you scared?"

Nancy said, "Yes I am, but I usually get over it after I start to sing."

"And all the people start to laugh," Marybelle said.

Plum said, "Nobody ever laughs at Nancy. She has a beautiful voice. Miss Waverly said so."

Marybelle said, "Who said anything about her voice. I'm talking about the way she looks. Her skirts are so short she looks like she's on stilts."

Plum said, "Well, that's better than looking like a dishmop and sounding like Donald Duck like you do."

Nancy said, "Please, Plum, let's do our work."

Marybelle said, "Please, Plum, let's do our work. Please, Plum, let's do our work."

Nancy said, "Come on, Plum, please. You know Marybelle is just trying to make trouble." She grabbed Plum's arm and tried to pull her through the swinging door to the pantry.

Plum said, "All right, but just wait till the program is over."

Marybelle stuck out her tongue and Plum made such a terrible face at her that even Nancy shivered. Then, her blue eyes blazing, Plum said, "When the program and the school picnic are over I'm going to pound Marybelle Whistle to jelly, and I don't care what Mrs. Monday does to me."

Nancy said, "And I'll help you but now please go out and get to work. You know Mrs. Monday will be here in a minute."

It was several hours later while Plum was watching the

chickens scratching around in their fresh straw and flying up to their clean roosts that she had her idea. Why not a chicken for a carrier pigeon? She'd attach the letter to its wing and throw it over the fence. It might fly over to another farm and another farmer might notice it and pick it up and might find the letter and might mail it.

It was a wonderful idea, Plum thought, so while Tom was working in the barn, she sneaked up on, and caught, one of the fat red hens. Carefully she tied the letter to its wing, then carried it out in back by the vegetable garden and threw it over the fence. With a terrified squawk the chicken flapped its wings and sailed to the ground. But instead of being glad of its freedom and flying away, as Plum had planned, it rushed over and began running along the fence trying to find a hole to squeeze through. Plum ran ahead of it and tried to shoo it away from the fence but the chicken paid no attention to her.

"Squawk, squawk, squawk," she croaked, running hysterically along the fence around the garden.

"Oh, you dummy," Plum moaned. "Go that way! Out toward the road."

But the hen ignored her and continued to poke her head between the pickets, jerk it out, run back farther and try again. When the lunch gong sounded she was still back by the orchard.

Plum told Nancy about the chicken at lunch and Nancy laughed so hard she choked on her potato soup and Mrs. Monday rapped on her glass for silence.

After lunch, when they were scrubbing off the front porch

and steps, Plum sneaked out in back to see how her carrier pigeon was doing. She couldn't find it. She walked the fence around the whole place but the chicken was gone. "Old Tom probably found it and put it back," Nancy said.

Plum said, "Well, in that case the letter is as good as burned, so I'm going right in now and ask Mrs. Monday to buy us new dresses for that program. I'll tell her it really doesn't matter so much about me because nobody cares how good spellers are dressed but singers have to look nice."

Nancy said, "I'll go with you."

Plum said, "No, because she might get mad and make me stay home and you just can't stay home, it would spoil the whole program."

Nancy said, "If I don't have a new dress I want to stay home." So they went in together and rapped on Mrs. Monday's sitting-room door.

Marybelle opened the door and said, "What do you two want?"

Plum said, "We want to see Mrs. Monday."

Marybelle said, "Well, she doesn't want to see you," and slammed the door.

Plum knocked again very loudly. There was no answer. She knocked again much louder and heard Mrs. Monday say, "Marybelle, for mercy's sake, answer the door."

Marybelle opened the door a tiny crack and Plum pushed past her and into the room. Nancy followed. Mrs. Monday, who was sitting by the window doing needlepoint, looked up at Plum and Nancy and said, "Well?"

Plum said, "Mrs. Monday, Nancy is going to sing a solo in the program at school and she just has to have a new dress. Her old school dress is so short she looks like a stork and her shoes are all worn out."

Mrs. Monday said, "I see no point in getting new school clothes at the end of the year. They'll be outgrown by the beginning of the fall term."

Plum said, "Mrs. Monday, Marybelle told us today that everyone will laugh at Nancy when she gets up to sing and she said that it wouldn't be because of her singing but because of her terrible old short school dress and worn-out shoes."

Mrs. Monday, eyes on her needlepoint, said, "I repeat that I see no point in purchasing new clothes at the end of the school year. If Nancy wishes to show off her singing ability that is her problem, not mine."

Plum said, "Mrs. Monday, would you want Marybelle to wear a short, worn-out dress to recite *Hiawatha?*"

Mrs. Monday said, "What Marybelle does or wears has nothing to do with you and Nancy. Marybelle has parents who are well able to provide for her."

Plum said, "But we have Uncle John."

Nancy said, "And I wrote to him today."

Mrs. Monday said, "Where is the letter?"

Nancy said, "I mailed it."

Mrs. Monday said, "And how, may I ask?"

Nancy said, "I won't tell you."

Mrs. Monday said, "Either you tell me, Nancy, or you and Plum will not go to the program or the picnic."

Nancy said, "I won't tell you. I won't! I won't! I won't! You're cruel and horrible and I hate you and we will go to the program." She burst into tears and ran out of the room slamming the door behind her.

Mrs. Monday turned to Plum and said, "Well, that settles that unless, of course, Pamela, you care to tell me how Nancy mailed her letter."

Plum said, "I won't tell you, Mrs. Monday. And no matter what you say or do, Nancy and I will go to the program and the picnic."

Mrs. Monday picked up her needlepoint, carefully inserted the needle, pulled it through to the back and said, "We shall see, Pamela. Now go to your room."

Plum turned and started across the room. Just as she got to the door, Marybelle, who had been standing by a table supposedly feeding her goldfish, but really listening to, and enjoying, the fracas, called to Plum and made a face at her. Plum, instead of making a face back at her as Marybelle had expected her to, looked at her for a minute, then walked over, picked up the goldfish bowl and put it, goldfish and all, down over Marybelle's head. Marybelle tried to scream but the sound that came out was more like rain water bubbling down a storm sewer. Mrs. Monday apparently didn't even hear her, so Plum sauntered slowly out of the room and closed the door carefully behind her.

Some of the other children, who had seen Nancy come storming out of the sitting room a few minutes before, clustered around Plum and asked what had happened. She said, "I'll tell you about it later," and ran upstairs.

She found Nancy lying on their bed sobbing convulsively. Plum sat down beside her and said, "Well, I feel better now. I jammed the goldfish bowl down over Marybelle's head. It had the goldfish in it, too."

Nancy turned over and said, "Did you really?"

Plum said, "Yes, I was trying to be like Sara Crewe and hold in my anger but Mrs. Monday was so horrible and cruel and that little sneak was standing there enjoying it all and pretending to feed her goldfish, and when I started to go out she called to me and then made a face at me and it wasn't a bad face at all, not half as bad as the ones I make or the ones she usually makes at me, but it was just too much. The next thing I knew the goldfish bowl was down over her head and there was seaweed all down the front of her and one big fat goldfish swimming around in her pocket."

Nancy wiped her swollen red eyes on her sleeve and said, "Didn't Marybelle scream?"

Plum said, "She gurgled like dishwater when the sink's stopped up. Mrs. Monday didn't even hear her, so I just sauntered out and closed the door."

Nancy said, "Well, we're certainly in trouble now. I wonder what Miss Waverly will say when I tell her we can't be in the program and can't go to the school picnic."

Plum said, "I don't care so much about the program but we are going to the picnic. We're going to run away and go."

Nancy said, "But how? You know that we'll be locked in."

Plum said, "I don't know how, but I'll find a way. Now I'm going down and try to find that dumb chicken. If Mrs.

Monday comes up, don't talk back to her. Just don't say anything to her." Plum went out.

In a few minutes, Eunice, Evangeline, Sally, Todd and Allan came in to see what had happened. When Nancy told them they all laughed delightedly at Plum's putting the goldfish bowl on Marybelle's head but they were furious at Mrs. Monday's unfairness.

Sally said, "I'm going to be a tree in the program and Miss Dowd made us all tree costumes and I don't see why, as long as you are going to sing 'Trees,' you couldn't wear one of those. They're awfully pretty. The dresses are long and brown and our arms and heads are all covered with pale pink blossoms."

Nancy said, "That's a wonderful idea, Sally. Do you think if I asked her, Miss Dowd would make me one?"

Sally said, "She wouldn't have to, there's an extra one because Jeanie Kirk has mumps and can't wear hers."

Eunice said, "I'll go with you Monday and we can ask Miss Waverly to ask Miss Dowd."

Nancy said, "Oh, I forgot. Mrs. Monday said that Plum and I can't be in the program and we can't go to the picnic."

Todd said, "She can't keep you out of a school program. That's against the law."

Allan said, "That's right. She can keep you home from the picnic but she wouldn't dare keep you out of the program."

Nancy said, "Are you sure?"

Todd said, "Yes, because at another boarding home where I was, the woman kept some of the bigger kids home from school to do the work and the truant officer came out and then the police came and they closed up her house and sent all the kids home."

Nancy said, "Was that out in the country like this?"

Todd said, "No, it was in Central City but I'm just sure you have to let kids go to school."

Plum came in then, looking very dejected, and said, "I can't find that old chicken. She must have flown back over the fence and gotten back with the other chickens."

Nancy said, "Never mind, Plum, Sally had a splendid idea," and she told Plum about the tree costume.

Plum said, "But Mrs. Monday said we couldn't be in the program."

Todd said, "I know but if you tell Miss Waverly that Mrs. Monday's going to keep you home for a punishment, she'll get the principal to talk to her."

Allan said, "Yeah, Plum, keeping kids out of school is against the law."

Plum said, "Oh, boy, do you think she'll get sent to jail?"

Todd said, "She might, if the truant officer catches her."

A voice from the doorway said, "Why are you children up here? Why aren't you doing your work?"

The children scattered like frightened birds and Mrs. Monday said, "Pamela, I expect you to apologize to Marybelle."

Plum said, "Mrs. Monday, I will apologize to Marybelle, if you let Nancy be in the school program."

Mrs. Monday said, "I do not bargain with children,

103

Pamela. When Nancy has apologized to me for her outrageous behavior I will then take the matter of the school program under consideration."

Nancy said, "Mrs. Monday, I'm sorry I lost my temper, that was very foolish of me, but you were unfair about the school clothes. I have worn the same school dress for two years and it is all faded and shabby and it is way, way above my knees."

Mrs. Monday said, "I feel that I was perfectly justified in telling you that it would be foolish to buy new school clothes at the end of the school year."

Nancy said, "But, Mrs. Monday, a new dress wouldn't be just for school. I could wear it to Sunday School, to Library Day and when company comes."

Mrs. Monday said, "I am the best judge of if and when you need new clothes. Now let's hear no more of this. Pamela, are you ready to come down and apologize to Marybelle?"

Plum said, "Mrs. Monday, if I apologize will you let Nancy go to the school program?"

Mrs. Monday said, "I repeat, Pamela, I do not bargain with children."

Plum said, "Then I won't apologize."

Mrs. Monday said, "Very well, then, you will both stay in your room until you do apologize." She went out, closing the door and locking it.

Plum said, "It's lucky she doesn't know how easy it is for me to go out the window and down the maple tree."

Nancy said, "Do you think Todd and Allan are right? Do

you think that Mrs. Monday has to let us be in the school program?"

Plum said, "Yes, but knowing Mrs. Monday, she'll figure out a way to keep us home and that is why I'm planning on running away the night before."

Nancy said, "But how will we get over the fence?"

Plum said, "I'll think of a way. You just wait and see. Now I'm going down the tree and ask Old Tom for some fresh milk."

Nancy stood by the window and watched Plum climb down the maple tree, take a quick look around to be sure no one was watching, then skitter across the barnyard and through the big barn door. Nancy saw St. Nick and her kittens come running up to Plum. "Oh, those darling kittens," she said. "I wonder how much they've grown."

She was squinting her eyes trying to see into the darkness of the barn, when suddenly she thought, "I'll go down and see the kittens. If Plum can go down the tree, so can I."

Rather timidly she eased herself out the window and onto the big limb that was just below the sill. With one hand she held to a branch over her head, with the other she clutched the window ledge. Then she looked down. My goodness, it was far down to the ground. She was right above one of the lightwells of the basement windows, too, and it was deep and dark and solid cement. Nancy shivered and looked longingly back into the little bedroom. Then she looked over toward the barn. She could still see Plum bent over playing with the kittens. Carefully she let go of the sill, moved her hand down to the branch beside her and inched her way along until she got to the main trunk. Still holding to the upper branch, she moved to a lower one. Then she changed hands and moved to a still lower one. It was scary but fun. She was surprised when she finally saw the ground just a few feet away. She jumped down, took a look around the way Plum had done and then skipped across the barnyard and slipped through the door calling, "Plum, I did it. I climbed down the tree."

Plum said, "Wow, you scared me. It wasn't hard, was it, Nancy?"

Nancy said, "At first I was nervous, especially when I looked down at the ground, but then I started down and the next thing I knew I was almost on the ground."

Plum said, "That's the way with everything the first time you do it. You're sort of shaky and your stomach feels awfully empty, that's the way I felt when I went in to ask Mrs. Monday for the new dresses, then you feel a little bit better and then before you know it, whatever it is you used to be afraid of, is over. Look at Prancer, he's the biggest."

Nancy said, "Come here, Prancer, don't you remember me?" She picked up the fat little kitten and held it against her cheek. Prancer began to purr very softly and Nancy, her tear-swollen eyes shining, said, "Oh, Plum, listen to him. He likes me."

Plum said, "Come over here, I'll show you how funny they are when they play. I've got a string with a piece of paper tied on it and when I drag it across the floor they all jump on it and on each other."

For about half an hour the little girls played with the kittens. Then Old Tom came in to milk and they stood and watched him and drank dipper after dipper of the warm foaming milk. Old Tom said, "No supper again tonight, eh? What's the trouble this time?"

Plum told him about the program and the scene in Mrs. Monday's sitting room and when she got to the part about the goldfish globe, Old Tom laughed so hard that Clover turned around to see what the commotion was.

Old Tom said, "Look, isn't that just like a woman? Curious as can be. Gotta know what the joke is. Now you turn around there, Clover, and concentrate on giving down your milk so these hungry little children can have some supper."

Plum said, "I love it out here in the barn. I wish we lived out here."

Old Tom said, "It can get mighty lonesome out here, Plum. I love animals and they're awfully comforting at times but it's pretty hard to stay out here alone in the winter, especially when your own sister is living in such style right across the barnyard."

"Your own sister, Mrs. Monday?" Both little girls said together.

"Yep," Tom said. "My own sister. This was our home when we were little kids. We jumped in the old haymow together. We both rode our ponies together. We went to school together. But when we grew up we went different ways. Mine wasn't a good way and I got in some serious trouble and when things got awful bad I turned to my sister Marybelle for help.

She helped me, I'll say that for her, but she never let me forget it. At first I was so troubled I didn't notice how things had changed around here. But after I had been back a year or two, I saw that my sister Marybelle had turned into a hard, greedy woman. A woman who lets nothing or nobody stand in her way. I don't know much about you two except that I like you and I feel sorry for you and if ever there's anything I can do to help you, that's in my power anyway and that my sister can't find out about, I'll sure do it."

Nancy and Plum thanked Old Tom, and Plum said, "Well, Tom, if Mrs. Monday won't let us go to the school program or the picnic, we are planning on going anyway and we may need you to help us get out."

Old Tom said, "I don't have the keys to the gates, she keeps them, but if she wasn't home I could help you over the fence."

Plum said, "If you help us, Tom, someday maybe we can help you."

Old Tom said, "Who knows, Plum, who knows?"

While Plum and Nancy and Old Tom were talking in the barn, a farmer had stopped his truck and was examining a dead chicken that he had found lying in the road.

"Too bad," he said. "Somebody's nice big, fat red hen."

He was just going to throw it in the ditch when he noticed something tied to its wing. Something white. With his pocketknife he cut the strings that held it, saw that the white thing was a letter, put the letter in his pocket and tossed the dead chicken away.

When he got home he told his wife about finding the chicken with the letter tied to its wing. His wife said, "Sounds like some child's idea. Let me see the letter."

The farmer took it out of the pocket of his blue shirt and handed it to his wife. She adjusted her glasses, looked it over carefully and said, "Certainly it is the work of a child. Notice the round careful writing. Also it hasn't any stamp. Well, I'm going to town tomorrow and I'll put a stamp on it and drop it at the post office."

8

Uncle John's Visit

MONDAY MORNING AT RECESS, Nancy and Plum asked Miss Waverly if she would ask Miss Dowd if Nancy could wear the extra tree costume, *if* she sang her solo.

Miss Waverly said, "What do you mean, *if* Nancy sings her solo?"

Nancy said, "Well, Mrs. Monday has told Plum and me that we can't be in the program or go to the picnic but we're hoping that she will change her mind and if she doesn't we're going to try and come anyway."

Miss Waverly said, "Why won't Mrs. Monday let you be in the program or come to the picnic?"

Nancy and Plum told her the whole story and when they

got through, Miss Waverly's cheeks were bright red, her eyes were flashing and her lips were set in a thin straight line. She said, "Nancy and Plum, you can just plan on being in the program and you can count on the picnic. I am going in to see the principal."

Nancy and Plum hugged each other and Nancy said, "And you know what else, Plum, if I wear a tree costume to sing, then you can wear my school dress for the spelling match and it won't be short on you at all."

Apparently Miss Waverly was as good as her word. That very afternoon when the children were changing their school clothes, Mrs. Monday sent Marybelle up to tell them that she had reconsidered and if Plum apologized to Marybelle they could be in the program and go to the picnic.

Marybelle said, "Aunty Marybelle said that if you apologize to me, Nancy can sing her ugly old song and you can spell all the words wrong at the program Friday. She said you can go to the picnic, too."

Plum said, "All right, Marybelle. I'm sorry I put that little goldfish bowl on your head. I wish it had been bigger and with a shark in it."

Marybelle said, "That isn't a real apology."

Plum said, "You didn't tell us what Mrs. Monday really said, either."

Marybelle said, "Oh, all right. She said that you and Nancy can be in the program and go to the picnic if you tell me you're sorry."

111

Plum said, "All right, I'm sorry"—adding under her breath, "that you're such a sneaky little tattletale."

Marybelle said, "What did you say, Plum?"

Plum said, "I said I'm sorry."

Marybelle said, "You said something more."

Plum said, "I was just practicing my spelling words."

Marybelle said, "I heard you say 'sneaky little tattletale'!"

Plum said, "Oh, Marybelle, you must have misunderstood me. I was spelling antique—a-n-t-i-q-u-e—and cattail—c-a-t-t-a-i-l. Those were two new words we had yesterday."

Marybelle said, "You didn't spell antique right—it's anteek."

Plum said, "It is not."

Marybelle said, "It is so."

Nancy said, "Come on, Plum, we must get started on our work. We have to wash all the parlor windows before supper."

Marybelle said, "A-n-t-i-q-u-e! That sounds crazy."

Plum said, "Just wait and see who wins the spelling match, Woodenhead with shaving curls."

Marybelle said, "I'm going to tell."

Plum said, "Oh, I forgot. I'm sorry, Marybelle, and you're right about antique—it's a-n-t-e-e-k."

Marybelle said, "Now who's a woodenhead?" Then she flounced out of the room.

Plum said, "I hope antique really is one of the words they give us."

Nancy said, "Come on, Plum, hurry. You know how long it takes to wash windows with cold water and ammonia."

Meanwhile, Mrs. Monday was in her sitting room tapping her foot, staring at the fire and boiling with rage. "How dare they tell me how to run my boarding home! 'If Nancy and Pamela Remson aren't at school Friday, I will take it up with the juvenile court,' he said. What troublemakers. What dreadful little troublemakers! They get worse every day."

Just then Marybelle came in to report that Plum had apologized. She said, "I made old Plum apologize and then we were practicing for the spelling contest on Friday and do you know how that old woodenhead of a Plum spelled antique— a-n-t-i-q-u-e?"

Mrs. Monday said, "And what is wrong with that?"

Marybelle said, "Wrong? Why, it should be spelled a-n-t-e-e-k, that's all."

Mrs. Monday said, "Oh, you stupid, stupid little girl. Go out of here."

Marybelle stared at her aunt in amazement. Never in all her life had she spoken to her like that.

She said, "Aunty Marybelle, you're being mean to me."

Mrs. Monday said, "Oh, get out of here. Hurry up. I'm trying to think."

Marybelle went out and stood around in the parlor watching Nancy and Plum wash the windows. She said, "There's a streak there. Look, that one's not clean. You're not getting the corners. You'll never finish by supper time."

Until Plum, irritated beyond endurance, said, "Oh, pardon me, honey," and splashed about a cupful of the ammonia water on Marybelle's head. It smelled and stung her eyes and Marybelle began to bawl, "You did that on purpose, Plum Remson. I'm going to tell."

Plum said, "Oh, Marybelle, I'm so sorry. Run out to the kitchen and wash your face with warm water."

Marybelle said, "I'm going to tell," and ran back into the sitting room.

She had just begun, "Aunty Marybelle, Plum . . ." when her Aunty Marybelle grabbed her by the shoulders and thrust her out of the room, saying, "I'm tired of your sniveling and tattling. Now go out and help the other children."

Plum, who had gone to the kitchen for clean cloths, heard her and was so delighted that she threw her sponge up in the air and it splatted against the ceiling and left a big round spot like a sun with rays coming out from it. Nancy said, "Mrs. Monday is certainly in a terrible temper. No matter how well we do the windows I'll bet she'll say they look streaky and take our supper away."

Plum said, "What do we care? Now that you can climb down the tree, we can go out and drink warm milk. I like it better than scorched oatmeal or beans with rocks in them, anyway."

Nancy said, "I wonder if grown people always have the joy taken out of things the way children do. I mean, I wonder if when you're grown up and you're going to do something that's going to be a lot of fun like a picnic, if you have to be reminded of it over and over and over, or if you have to do extra work to earn it or if after it is over you have to be told every day that you have had your fun for that month."

Plum said, "Well, the grown people I know aren't nearly as happy as children, so I guess it must be worse after you grow up."

Nancy said, "I certainly hope that tree costume will cover my worn-out shoes."

Plum said, "Why don't you take off your shoes and then your brown socks will look just like part of your costume?"

Nancy said, "That is a good idea and not wearing shoes will make the costume longer, too."

Plum said, "I don't know what I'm going to do about my shoes. The holes in the soles are so big they won't even hold paper any more. It's just like going barefoot and you know how slivery the platform is."

Nancy said, "Oh, well, Plum, it's like you said. People don't care how good spellers are dressed, how worn out their shoes are."

Plum said, "Well, with my shoes and the way I look the words are going to have to be awfully hard."

Nancy said, "I'll bet old Marybelle has a new dress and brand new party shoes."

Plum said, "I bet she does, too, and I hope she misses the very first word."

Nancy said, "Now, my side's all finished. Do they look awfully streaky?"

Plum said, "No, they look as clear and sparkly as rain-drops. How do mine look?"

Nancy said, "Well, there are a few cloudy places. Here, I'll help you. Hand me that clean cloth."

Nancy was just wiping off the last streak on Plum's side when Mrs. Monday came in to inspect the windows and announce supper. The girls could tell the kind of a mood she was in because her eyes were so pale they were almost white, her mouth was so tight her lips had disappeared completely and her nostrils were quivering. Without a word she stalked around the long room and examined the windows. Then she noticed the spot on the ceiling.

She said, "How did that spot get up there?"

Plum said, "I dropped my sponge."

Mrs. Monday said, "You dropped your sponge up in the air?"

Plum said, "Well, it slipped out of my hand and flew up there."

Mrs. Monday said, "That was deliberate carelessness on your part, Pamela. You may go to your room. You will not have any supper."

Nancy said, "Don't the windows look nice, Mrs. Monday?"

Mrs. Monday said, "They certainly do not. The outsides are all spotty."

Nancy said, "You didn't tell us to wash the outside. You said to do the inside today and the outside tomorrow."

Mrs. Monday said, "I did no such thing. I told you to wash the parlor windows after school today."

Nancy said, "But, Mrs. Monday, we always do the inside one day and the outside the next day. Anyway, we couldn't do the outside, too, before supper. We only just finished the inside."

Mrs. Monday said, "Well, then perhaps you had better not have any supper. Perhaps you had better wash the outside of the windows, as you were told to do, while the other children are eating their supper."

Nancy said, "You're very unfair, Mrs. Monday. You're unkind and unfair."

Mrs. Monday shouted. "NANCY REMSON, BE QUIET!" And Nancy was so frightened that she was.

Old Tom helped Nancy move the stepladder around to the different windows and as he moved it she told him about Mrs. Monday's unfairness. He said, "She's a woman who will not tolerate being crossed. She'll do anything to get her own way. Anything."

While the other children were having their supper, Tom brought Nancy a fruit jar of warm milk and told her that Plum was in the barn playing with the kittens. He said, "Plum feels awful bad because she isn't helping you but she's afraid to let Mrs. Monday know that she's out."

Nancy said, "Tell her not to worry. I can stand anything now that I know I'm going to be in the program and am going to the picnic."

And for the next four days Mrs. Monday certainly put her to the test. Plum, too, of course.

Every morning, on each child's door was tacked a list of their daily duties. On Nancy and Plum's door the list was so long and contained so many extra duties that in order to accomplish them they had to get up at dawn and work until almost midnight.

Mrs. Monday ordered them to clean out the attic and scrub the splintery floor; clean up the basement, even the coalbin and scrub the floor; clean and sweep out a spidery, dark, dusty toolshed; clean out and sweep the woodshed; wash all the dishes from every meal; cut the lawns; trim the hedges and weed the garden. She took away all their meals but the lunch they had at school and every morning she sent them on so many errands they almost missed the school bus.

Thursday afternoon, as they got off the bus, Nancy said, "I'm so tired I don't even care about the program and the picnic tomorrow."

Plum said, "I'm so tired I can't even remember how to spell cat. How can anybody be as cruel and hateful as Mrs. Monday?"

Nancy said, "I wonder what hard, dirty, tiresome, awful job she will have for us this afternoon."

Plum said, "Probably make us clean out the chimneys or wash off the roofs with our tongues."

Slowly, wearily they went up the front steps and into the front hall as Mrs. Monday came out of her sitting room. To their astonishment she was smiling and to their further astonishment she said, "No extra work this afternoon, girls. Just go up to your room and rest. You are going to have a big day tomorrow and you'll need your strength."

Plum and Nancy just stood and stared. So Mrs. Monday took each of them by a thin, bony little shoulder and gave them a playful little push toward the stairs, saying, "Go on, girls, go up and rest. Don't just stand there staring."

A few minutes later, as they lay stretched out exhausted on their bed, Nancy said, "I can't believe it. She said for us to rest—not to weed the lawn or sweep out the barn or chop a cord of wood, but to rest."

Plum said, "She must be going to kill us and she wants us to look nice in our coffins."

Nancy said, "Or, maybe she's sorry she's been so horrible."

Plum said, "If you're as horrible as Mrs. Monday, you don't even know you're horrible. Anyway, she doesn't act sorry. She acts glad about something."

Nancy said, "Well, I don't care why she's being nice. I'm just glad she is."

Plum said, "I do. I want to know what's going on but I'm too tired to sneak around and find out."

It's just as well that Plum did rest because no matter how hard she tried she couldn't have found out the reason for the change in Mrs. Monday. Nobody knew but Mrs. Monday and she felt just like a cat that has finally caught two very annoying little mice. You see, that day while the children were at school, Uncle John had telephoned.

He had said, "Mrs. Monday, I just received a letter from my niece Nancy. A most upsetting letter. She tells me that she and Pamela are to be in a program at school and they need new shoes and new dresses. She also tells me that she has written me several times before but guesses that I have been too busy to answer. What I want to know, Mrs. Monday, is what has happened to all the money I have given you for new clothes for the girls and why haven't I received Nancy's other letters?"

As she listened to Uncle John, Mrs. Monday's eyes flashed, little bubbles of spit formed in the corners of her mouth and her face turned from ashen to raspberry color and finally to navy blue. She was more furiously angry than she had ever been in her life. However, Mrs. Monday was not one to let anything stand in her way, even anger, so with a great and visible effort she composed herself, smiled her mirthless smile and turned her face back to its normal greenish olive hue. Her voice was perfectly controlled when she spoke to Uncle John. She said, "Now, my dear, dear Mr. Remson, I wouldn't be upset if I were you. You know how little girls are. I saw the letter that Nancy wrote to you but I let her mail it because I hoped that a man of your intelligence and experience would realize that it was just one of those foolish, childish outbursts of Nancy's that I have tried so hard to teach her to control. Of course, the girls have beautiful clothes, Mr. Remson. You have always given me plenty of money to buy them everything they need but, as much as I hate to have to say this, some children are never satisfied. You can buy some children everything in the world, a new dress every day, and still they want more. I have tried again and again to explain to Nancy and Pamela that having more than the other children is liable to cause hard feelings. But nothing seems to affect them, so I let Nancy write to you and try and wheedle you into giving in to them. Now, I'm terribly sorry that I didn't handle the situation right here. It was very thoughtless of me. But really, Mr. Remson, I deal with children so much that I suppose I expect everyone to react to them the way I do. To laugh at their childish greediness and vanity. Again I say I am very, very sorry that this happened."

Uncle John said, "Well, I suppose I was silly to get upset, but this is the first letter I have ever had from Nancy. What do you suppose happened to the others she wrote me?"

Mrs. Monday said, "Probably forgot to mail them, or was careless about the address. You know how children are."

Uncle John said, "Well, anyway I think I'll come out and see the children. They must be getting pretty big now, probably almost ready for boarding school."

Mrs. Monday said quickly, "Oh, Mr. Remson, not boarding school! Nancy and Pamela are still babies and will need a mother's understanding and care for a long time yet."

Uncle John said, "Well, I'll see. When would be the best time to come out and talk to the girls?"

Mrs. Monday said, "Come Friday, Mr. Remson. It is the last day of school and the children will be home early."

Uncle John said, "Very well. Friday afternoon about four-thirty."

Mrs. Monday said, "Splendid. I'll be looking forward to it and I know how delighted Nancy and Pamela will be."

She hung up the phone and picked up her needlepoint and no hawk that had just finished eating two baby chickens ever looked more satisfied.

The next morning when Nancy and Plum jumped out of bed at the first clang of the morning bell, they were surprised not to find the usual long list of extra duties pinned to the outside of their door.

"Oh, gosh," Plum said. "Katie forgot to put our list up and I'll have to go down and get it."

Nancy said, "The first one dressed will go down and get it. Let's race."

But when Nancy, who was dressed first, went down to the kitchen Katie told her that Mrs. Monday had ordered "no extra duties for anyone. Not only that," Katie said, "but she told me to fix an extra big lunch as she didn't expect you home from the picnic until dark."

When Nancy told Plum this wonderful news, Plum said, "Miss Waverly and the principal must have really scared her. Oh, boy, I hope she goes to jail."

Nancy said, "Well, as long as we have plenty of time, I'll go down to the washroom and iron my school dress for you."

Plum said, "But what will you wear to school?"

Nancy said, "I'm going to wear my play clothes. They'll do for the picnic and I'll have on a costume for the program."

Plum said, "Look how nice our shoes look. I rubbed them with bacon grease and tied the knots in the shoelaces underneath so they don't show."

Nancy said, "They look awfully nice but won't they get all dusty?"

Plum said, "We'll carry them until we get on the school bus. I've put our clean socks inside them."

Nancy said, "Wouldn't it be wonderful if we had new black patent-leather party shoes, new ruffled petticoats and new dresses with full skirts that would stand straight out when we whirled?"

Plum said, "And our hair curled and a bath in bubble bath?"

Eunice came in their room then, stuck up her foot and said, "Look, my whole sole just came loose."

Plum said, "Well, at least you've got one to come loose. Look at my shoes." She held up her greasy brown oxfords and showed Eunice the soles which gaped with holes as big as butter plates. She said, "I just made new soles out of my arithmetic notebook but I know they won't last all day."

Nancy said, "Oh, well, after today we can go barefoot. Now I have to go down and iron that dress."

At breakfast, Nancy and Plum noted with envy that Marybelle wore a new pale pink dress with a sash, a full, full skirt and a ruffled petticoat and she had on brand new black patent-leather slippers.

Plum said, "Usually I'm glad I'm smart but today I'd rather be as dumb as Marybelle and have a new dress and new shoes just like hers."

Nancy said, "Let's not look at her. Let's think about Lookout Hill and Miss Waverly and all the fun we are going to have."

Plum said, "I'm going to climb one of those great big enormous pine trees on top of Lookout Hill and then I am going to look around and see the whole world."

Nancy said, "I'm going to gather pine cones and pick bluebells and try and find a real, little mountain brook."

Eunice said, "I'm taking Nanela to the picnic and I'm going to make a wreath of flowers for her hair."

Todd said, "I'm going to throw a rock from the top of

Lookout Hill into that river way down there in the canyon. I bet that's about a million feet."

Mrs. Monday said, "Come, come, children, hurry with your breakfast, it is almost time for the school bus."

When Nancy and Plum got on the school bus carrying their shoes and socks, Mr. Harris said, "Won't she let you wear your shoes in the house any more?"

Plum said, "Oh, certainly we can wear shoes but I just polished these with bacon grease and I didn't want them to get all dusty."

Mr. Harris said, "Here, I'll put 'em up here by me. You did a good job of polishing. They look almost brand new."

Plum said, "Just take a look at the soles."

Mr. Harris turned the oxfords over and when he saw the huge gaping holes he said, "Well, shoes with holes in 'em are better than no shoes. What's this writing on the inside, 'How much carpet would it take to cover a floor 12' x 15'7"'?"

Plum said, "Oh, I made new soles out of my arithmetic notebook."

Mr. Harris said, "Well, that was a good idea. Now you have brains in your feet as well as your head, which is more than I can say about some people," he added as Marybelle pranced down the aisle, her curls bouncing, her new full skirt swishing.

Nancy said, "Gosh, Marybelle looks beautiful."

Mr. Harris said, "Well, in my opinion it takes more than fine feathers to make a fine bird. I also say that beauty is as beauty does and as far as I'm concerned even if Marybelle Whistle was dressed entirely in diamonds and emeralds, she still wouldn't hold a candle to you two."

Nancy said, "Oh, but, Mr. Harris, look at our old fadey clothes and our hard ugly pigtails."

Mr. Harris said, "That isn't what I see when I look at you, Nancy. I see a little girl with red hair, my favorite color, sweet dreamy gray eyes, gentle ways and dimples around her mouth. A beautiful little girl. One I'd be proud to have for my daughter."

Plum said, "What do you see when you see me?"

Mr. Harris said, "I see two yellow pigtails, my favorite color, big laughing blue eyes, a merry mouth that's quick to answer back and a child that's got so much spirit that she glows. A beautiful little girl. One I'd be proud to have for my own."

Plum said, "What do you see when you see Marybelle?"

Mr. Harris said, "I better get this school bus started or we'll all be late to school."

Miss Waverly had Nancy's tree costume all ready for her and to distinguish her from the other trees, she and Miss Dowd had made Nancy's headdress and branches out of white dogwood blossoms. Nancy looked so beautiful in her costume that when she began to sing:

> "I think that I shall never see
> A poem lovely as a tree,"

Miss Waverly and Miss Dowd had to wipe tears out of their eyes and Mr. Harris blew his nose so loud he almost drowned out the music.

The only mishap in the program was when Plum won the spelling match. She got so excited she kicked her foot in the air and little pieces of her arithmetic notebook jumped out of the hole in the bottom of her shoe and fluttered all over the stage like white moths. All the children laughed and Plum's face got as red as fire and Nancy was afraid she might be going to cry. Then Miss Waverly hissed at her, "Laugh, Plum. They think it is part of the program." So Plum laughed and kicked up the other foot and scattered more papers and everyone clapped and clapped.

The picnic was perfect. Not in the least like Miss Gronk's. Miss Waverly skipped and laughed and talked with the children. Even took a swing on Plum's branch, although she really was too heavy and the branch thumped her up and down on the ground.

When they got to the top of Lookout Hill, Miss Waverly let them all try to throw stones down into the river before they had their lunch. After lunch they played games, had throwing contests, took walks, gathered wildflowers and pine cones, fed the squirrels, climbed trees, looked for gold and pretended they were explorers.

It was while they were being explorers looking for water that they heard the noise in the underbrush as though some animal were running away. It could have been a deer of course, but the children wanted it to be something more exciting, so

Miss Waverly said that it probably was either a big black bear or a mountain lion. All the little girls shivered and squealed and held hands and the little boys swaggered around pretending they had guns, saying, "Just let an ole bear come around me, that's all I ask." Or, "I bet I could hit a mountain lion right between the eyes with this big rock, just like this, see."

Miss Waverly told the boys that because they were so fearless and brave they had better walk ahead of the girls on the way back to the lookout point. Of course, the boys hid behind trees and jumped out roaring like lions or climbed up on high rocks and screamed like eagles. It was wild, exciting fun made more so by the fact that Miss Waverly didn't care how loud they yelled.

When they grew tired they threw themselves down on the springy pungent pine needles and shading their eyes with their arms stared up through the hairy arms of the pines to the clear blue sky.

"How far away is the sky?" Eunice asked and one of the boys answered quickly, "The nearest star is twenty-five trillion, five hundred billion miles away."

An eagle appeared in the sky, sailing in slow majestic circles, and then right after him an aeroplane, the sunlight on its silver body like slivers of glass.

Plum said, "I feel sorry for that eagle. He used to be the king of all this sky and now aeroplanes come roaring through all the time and compared to an aeroplane an eagle is like a gnat."

Nancy said, "I hate eagles. They eat baby birds and baby mice."

Plum said, "Well, look at people. They eat baby sheep and baby cows."

Miss Waverly said, "All of life is a contest. The weak against the strong—the stupid against the clever—the honest against the dishonest."

Plum said, "And Nancy and me against Mrs. Monday."

Miss Waverly said, "Plum, haven't you and Nancy ever seen your uncle since he left you at Mrs. Monday's?"

Plum said, "No. I guess he doesn't care much about us." Then suddenly she remembered about the Christmas box. She looked to be sure Marybelle was not within hearing, then told Miss Waverly about it.

Miss Waverly said, "Of course, Pamela, Mrs. Monday could be telling the truth but I think I'd write and ask your uncle about it."

Plum said, "We have written to Uncle John but he never answers the letters."

Miss Waverly said, "Do you have the right address?"

Plum said, "Of course, but we've always given the letters to Mrs. Monday to mail and maybe she didn't mail them."

Miss Waverly said, "Oh, I think she mailed your letters. Your uncle is probably a very busy man."

Plum said, "Well, just in case she didn't mail our other letters, I mailed our last one a new way. I tied it to a chicken."

Miss Waverly laughed and said, "Tied it to a chicken? What do you mean?"

So Plum told her about her carrier pigeon idea and how the chicken had disappeared.

Miss Waverly said, "I think an easier way to mail your letter would have been to take it to school and let me mail it for you."

Plum said, "We didn't like to bother you."

Miss Waverly said, "Well, anyway the program is over now, Nancy looked beautiful in her tree costume, you won the spelling match and here we are on Lookout Hill. Even Uncle John couldn't have improved this day."

Plum said, "Except I wouldn't mind having a pair of new shoes."

Miss Waverly said, "Oh, well, in summer you go barefoot all the time anyway."

Plum said, "It's just that Nancy and I would like to know that somebody really cares about us."

Miss Waverly said, "Well, Plum, dear, I do and I know that Miss Appleby does. That's two people."

Plum said, "But you're gone all summer and we only get to see Miss Appleby once a month on Library Day."

Miss Waverly said, "Oh, well, in summer you have the birds and the flowers and the trees and the crickets and the fireflies and Buttercup's calf. You don't need people. My goodness, it must be getting late. See how dark the shadows have grown. Go round up the children, Plum, we had better be starting back."

But when the children were rounded up, Eunice couldn't find her doll. She said that she remembered leaving Nanela on the parapet looking at the view while she and Nancy picked wildflowers. She said, "She wasn't there when I came back and I thought Molly or one of the other children was playing with her."

Miss Waverly and all the children began a hunt for Nanela but they couldn't find her. They went way back to the mountain stream. They searched on every little trail. They looked behind rocks, under trees, everywhere. It was quite dark and Eunice was crying when finally Marybelle shouted that she had found Nanela in the brush just to the left of the place where Eunice had left her.

Eunice said, "Oh, thank you, thank you, Marybelle. You were wonderful to find her."

Plum said, "It seems funny to me that Nanela should be in a place where nobody but Marybelle went."

Miss Waverly said, "Now, Plum, let's not be suspicious. Maybe Nanela fell off the wall. There was so much rough play this afternoon."

Plum said, "If Nanela had fallen off the wall she would have been in that river way down there. I think Marybelle hid her."

Marybelle, whose normally gray face had suddenly turned quite red, said, "I did not. I did not. I did not."

Miss Waverly said, "Come on now, children. Gather up the baskets and let's race down the hill to the sign. The first one down gets the last two cupcakes."

Even though they ran all the way down the hill and even though it was June, it was very dark by the time the school bus deposited the children in front of Mrs. Monday's.

As they went in the gate, Plum said, "Look at the taillights

131

of that car going down the road. They look like the eyes of a dragon."

Nancy said, "I wonder if that could be Old Tom going out to look for us."

Plum said, "Watch the dragon going up the hill. See how his fiery breath lights the way."

Marybelle said, "You kids are so silly. That isn't any dragon. That is your Uncle John's car."

Nancy said, "Our Uncle John's car? How do you know?"

Marybelle said, "Because Aunty Marybelle told me so this morning. She said that he was coming out this afternoon at four and for me to see that Miss Waverly didn't bring you home early. That's why I hid Eunice's doll."

Lowering her head, Plum butted Marybelle as hard as she could in the stomach.

Marybelle went "Ugh" and sat down on the grass.

Plum said, "You sneak, you horrible little sneak. Why didn't you tell us Uncle John was coming?"

Marybelle, who had quite a time getting her breath, began to snivel and said, "Because Aunty Marybelle told me not to. She told me she would spank me if I told."

Plum said, "Well, a spanking would be better than what I'm going to do to you."

Nancy said, "You're not going to do anything to her. You're coming in with me to see Mrs. Monday." She grabbed Plum's arm and jerked her up the front steps, through the front door and to the door of Mrs. Monday's sitting room. Nancy raised her hand to rap. The door opened and Mrs. Monday, smiling broadly, said, "Did you have a nice time today, girls?"

Nancy said, "Why didn't you tell us Uncle John was coming?"

Mrs. Monday said, "It must have slipped my mind. Anyway, didn't you tell me that nothing would keep you home from the picnic?"

Nancy said, "Mrs. Monday, Uncle John is our only relative and we have been waiting over six years to see him."

Mrs. Monday said, "You see, if you hadn't carried tales to school and made trouble for me with the principal, you would have been home here when your uncle arrived."

Plum said, "Oh, no we wouldn't, Mrs. Monday. You would have arranged it some way."

Mrs. Monday said, "Your uncle was terribly disappointed. He waited and waited."

Then Marybelle came in rubbing her stomach and crying, "Plum butted me in the stomach. I think she's broken some bones."

Plum said, "You don't have bones in your stomach, Woodenhead."

Mrs. Monday said, "Go in and wash your face, Marybelle. Pamela and Nancy, go to your room."

When Plum and Nancy got upstairs, all the children were waiting outside their door to hear what Mrs. Monday had said.

To their surprise, Plum asked them please to go away and

she and Nancy went inside and shut the door. As soon as the door was closed, Plum spread a handkerchief out on the bed and began going through her drawers, gathering up all her small treasures and tossing them in the handkerchief.

"What are you doing?" Nancy asked.

Plum carefully laid a large dried june bug and an empty snake's skin on top of her blue beads and said, "I'm gathering up my things. We are running away tonight."

9

The Escape

PLUM WHISPERED, "Just sit on the window sill for a minute, Nancy, until your eyes get used to the dark, then I'll tell you exactly where to put your feet. I'm so used to going up and down this old tree, I could do it with my eyes closed."

Nancy said, "But my bundle of treasures is so bulgy I don't think I can hold on to it and a branch, too."

Plum said, "Here, hand it to me. I'll take them both down and put them under the tree and then I'll come back up and help you."

Rather timidly and holding tightly to the edge of the window with one hand, Nancy leaned forward and handed Plum her bundle. Plum grabbed it and disappeared into the maple tree.

"How can Plum be so brave?" Nancy said to herself as she looked down fearfully into the deep scary darkness below her dangling legs. It was a very quiet night and the air was so heavy with the fragrance of summer that she felt as though she could reach out and get a handful of it.

The back door opened, squeak! shut, bang! and Nancy could almost see Katie reaching out with her fat red arms to get the mop. The pale yellow moon came up behind the barn and for a moment or two silhouetted the weathervane against it like an evil sign. The back door opened and shut again and Nancy knew that Katie had put the mop back, standing it upright with its thick strings flopped forward like a woman who has just washed her hair. Somewhere an owl said, "Whoo, whoo," and far down the valley a dog began to howl at the moon. Nancy shivered and wished Plum would hurry.

Then suddenly at her feet she heard Plum whisper, "Nancy, hurry, I just saw Mrs. Monday go into the front hall and she may be coming up to our room."

Nancy listened and sure enough, down the long hallway she could hear the approaching slap, slap of Mrs. Monday's big black oxfords.

Plum said, "Here, hand me your foot. Now hang on to the window sill and turn around. See, I'm putting your foot on a big limb. Now reach above you and grab the branch that is just over your head. Hurry!"

Nancy did as she was told and with Plum guiding her, in a matter of seconds, was in by the trunk beside Plum and screened from the house by the thick maple leaves.

Plum said, "I hope she only opens the door a crack and shines her flashlight on the bed. Those two bundles of old clothes we put under the covers do look like us asleep but I keep thinking what if she goes over and tries to shake one of them by the shoulders."

Nancy said, "Shhh, I hear her opening the door."

Creak went the door. Slap, slap went Mrs. Monday's feet. The beam of her flashlight skimmed across the wall. Then for one terrible minute Mrs. Monday's gaunt black shape was framed in the window. She stood quietly, apparently looking out. Then lowering the sash a little, she turned and went out.

Plum said, "I wonder if she knows."

Nancy said, "I don't think so. Otherwise she wouldn't have closed the window just a little. She would have shut it all the way or left it open."

Plum said, "Well, whether she knows or not, we've got to hurry. Can you see all right now, Nancy?"

Nancy said, "I can see everything."

Plum said, "Then follow me. Put your hands and feet just where I do and we'll be down in a minute." And they were.

They jumped the last few feet, picked up their bundles and as silently as shadows ran across the barnyard, slipped up the outside stairway and knocked on Old Tom's door.

"Who's there? What do you want?" Old Tom shouted, his voice frighteningly loud in the thick quiet.

"Hush, Tom," Plum hissed at the crack of the door. "It's us."

Old Tom opened the door and Plum and Nancy stepped

137

back into the shadows away from the revealing rectangle of yellow light.

Plum whispered, "Tom, come down to the barn. We're running away and we need help."

Old Tom quickly closed the door behind him and said, "Running away? What's this all about? I thought you went to the picnic."

Plum said, "We can't talk here. Come on down to the barn."

They crept down the stairs and slipped into the barn and then by lantern light, in the safety of Clover's stall, Nancy and Plum told him about the picnic and Uncle John's visit.

He said, "If I didn't think you were right, I'd tell you so. But I do think you should run away. It's the only way you'll ever get to see your uncle and learn the truth. The gates are all locked but if we take the big ladder out in back by the garden, I think I can help you over the fence. We'll have to blow out the lantern and work in the dark though. Come on."

Tom showed them where the ladder was and blew out the lantern. Then quietly, carefully he eased the long ladder through the door and carried it, with the little girls' help, around the barn, out to the garden and stood it against the fence almost straight up and down so that a good third of it extended up in the air beyond the sharp iron pickets.

"Now," he said, "you girls climb up clear to the top and hang on tight. Plum, you go first."

They climbed up, up toward the moon, holding tight to

their little bundles and gripping the round, far-apart rungs with their worn-out shoes. They were trembling a little when they got to the top but they could see for miles and miles across the moon-washed valley to the smudgy black hills.

Old Tom hissed, "Hold on tight, now, you're coming down." Slowly and carefully he lifted his end of the ladder. Down they came like performers on a trapeze at the circus. When the ladder was level, Tom told them to turn around and face him, then walking forward and moving his hands from rung to rung, he let them down on the other side. When he was holding to the rung closest to the fence, he told them to hang by their hands and drop. Plum went first. Nancy threw her down the treasures. Then Nancy let herself down between the last two rungs of the ladder, hung for a minute and let go. She landed half sitting down, but it didn't hurt.

Plum grabbed her hands and jerked her to her feet and danced her around and around in a circle as she sang, "Nancy, Nancy, we're free, we're free. We'll never go back to Mrs. Mondeeee!"

Then they ran up to the fence, reached through, shook Tom's hand and said, "Thank you, Tom. Thank you."

Tom said, "There's a farm about three or four miles up the road toward town that's got a big haystack in the field. It would be a nice place to sleep. Just climb up on top of it and burrow in. Now I better be getting back before *she* smells a rat."

Nancy said, "Don't worry, Tom, if we get work in town we'll come and see you."

Tom said, "Are you going to work, Nancy?"

She said, "Yes, we're going to work until we have enough money to go to Central City and see Uncle John."

He said, "What kind of work could little kids like you do?"

Nancy said, "Oh, baby sitting, dish washing . . ."

Plum said, "Carpentering, coal shoveling, lawn mowing . . ."

Old Tom said, "Well, good luck, girls, and here's a couple of dollars just in case you don't find work right away." He took two crumpled dollar bills out of his pocket and pushed them through the fence.

Plum said, "Oh, I'm sorry, Tom, but we couldn't take your money."

Nancy said, "Thank you just the same, Tom, but we're going to earn our own money."

Old Tom said, "Well, good-bye, good luck."

Plum and Nancy said, "Good-bye," then turned and went skipping off through the fields toward the road.

Plum said, "I feel just like a canary that's gotten out of its cage."

Nancy said, "I feel like a baby bird that is just going to fly. Oh, Plum, Plum, we're free. We'll never have to see Mrs. Monday again."

Plum said, and her voice was a wail, "Oh, I forgot. I was going to pound Marybelle to jelly before I left. I almost feel like going back."

Nancy said, "You don't. You wouldn't go back to Mrs. Monday's just to get even with that little grub."

Plum said, "Oh, I guess not. But when I think of her

hiding Eunice's doll and deliberately making us miss Uncle John I get so mad my stomach aches."

Nancy said, "Oh, Plum, let's wave to Mrs. Monday's. . . . Doesn't it look dark and dreary and unfriendly?"

They turned and waved their little bundles at the Boarding Home. It was all dark except for a few squiggles of light seeping out around the drawn draperies in Mrs. Monday's suite.

Plum said, "Good-bye, ugly, horrible, cruel, deceitful, dishonest Mrs. Monday! Good-bye, Woodenhead with the shaving curls Marybelle. I hope we never see you again."

Nancy said, "I feel badly about leaving Eunice and the other children but I do think it is for the best. Now that we're free we may be able to help them."

Plum said, "Last one to that little bridge is an earwig."

Nancy said, "Get on your marks, get set, go."

Like a streak, the children raced down the road, their flying feet in the dust as quick and noiseless as raindrops. They reached the bridge at the same time and pounded across, their footsteps going boom, boom, boom. It was like running across a drum. So they ran back and forth and back and forth until finally, breathless and gasping, they fell against the railing.

There was a small stream running through the little gully below the bridge and when they had quieted down, they could hear the *plurk, plurk, shshshsh* of the water pouring over stones and wriggling along over the pebbles.

Plum tossed a stone into the stream and it went *plink*. She said, "Someday I'd like to have a little stream right beside my bedroom so that at night I could lie in bed and listen to its funny little clurky, spinky noises."

Nancy said, "I'd like to live beside the sea so I could hear the *swishshshsh, boom* of the surf. I've never seen the ocean but I know exactly how it will look and smell and sound."

Plum said, "Night is funny. It's scary when you're inside but its soft and beautiful and fun when you're out in it."

Nancy said, "Oh, look, the lights of a car. We had better hide quick. Come on."

They scrambled down the bank and crouched on the ground under the bridge. The earth smelled old and damp, the little brook sounded as loud as a torrent, and when the car went over the old loose planks there was such a terrible splintering, crashing roar that the girls put their hands over their ears in terror.

"It doesn't sound to me as if that bridge is going to last another day," Plum said as she climbed up the bank.

Nancy said, "Boy, I don't want to be under it when it caves in. Come on, let's get started toward that farm."

So they walked and they walked and they walked. Once they saw a deer standing in an old orchard and he was as still as the trees. Once, right above their heads, a screech owl ripped the night to pieces with his strangled shriek. Once a rabbit almost hopped on their feet. Once a black mound behind a fence suddenly erupted with terrifying, snorting noises and turned out to be a cow. Once a little dog came running out at them, yipping and snarling ferociously, but when Plum

142

pointed her finger at him and said, "Be quiet!" he turned and fled back across the fields shrieking in terror.

It was a night of adventure. A night to remember.

Plum said, "You know, Nancy, we're really awfully lucky. Not many children ever have a chance to take walks in the nighttime."

Nancy said, "I know it. If children could only learn to know the nighttime and be friends with it they wouldn't be afraid in the dark."

Plum said, "I like the way things look different at night. See that tree there. What does it look like to you?"

Nancy said, "It looks like an Indian shooting a bow and arrow."

Plum said, "To me it looks like a Roman driving his chariot."

Nancy said, "What does that stump look like?"

Plum said, "It looks like a soldier wearing one of those tall fur hats."

Nancy said, "It looks like a mug with a handle."

Plum said, "What about that little aspen tree in the moonlight?"

Nancy said, "It looks like a little princess in a silver spangled cape."

Plum said, "That's just what I was going to say."

Nancy said, "Let's play 'rhymes.' I'll start. I'm walking along."

Plum said, "Singing a song."

Nancy said, "I'll never be wrong."

Plum said, "Until I hear the gong."

Nancy said, "Ding, ding, dong."

Plum said, "Saying so long."

Nancy said, "Don't stick in that prong."

Plum said, "I'm old and not yong."

Nancy said, "That's not a very good rhyme. Young with prong."

Plum said, "Well, there isn't anything else. Now let's play what Johnny has in his pocket. I'm going to start. Johnny has a marble in his pocket."

Nancy said, "Johnny has a marble and an apple in his pocket."

Plum said, "Johnny has a marble and an apple and a knife in his pocket."

Nancy said, "Johnny has a marble and an apple and a knife and a frog in his pocket."

Johnny had a marble and an apple and a knife and a frog and a pencil and a stick and a penny and a pin and a piece of gum and a handkerchief and a nail and an orange and a candle and a top and a ball and a slingshot in his pocket when Plum saw far over in a field an enormous lump that looked as if it might be the haystack.

She said, "Nancy, there it is. The haystack. Over there."

Nancy said, "I certainly hope it doesn't come to life and turn out to be a bull."

Plum said, "That's much bigger than a bull. It would have

to turn into a whale. Come on, let's climb over the fence and find out."

So they climbed over the fence, which was made of rails, and would have been very easy to climb if it hadn't been for the wild roses growing along it. Wild roses that smelled like warm cinnamon but whose thorny hands clutched frantically at Nancy and Plum and left long red scratches on their arms and legs.

After disentangling themselves from the roses, the children raced across the fields toward the haystack. The grass was new and lush and springy and so pleasant to feet in worn-out shoes that every few feet Plum jumped straight up in the air and Nancy took big giant steps that were really leaps.

The haystack was large. About fifteen feet high and as big around as a room. About as big around as a room at the top, that is. The bottom had been eaten away by the cows.

Plum said, "It looks like a giant mushroom. I wonder how we're going to get up on top of it."

Nancy said, "Let's walk all the way around it. Perhaps there is a ladder or something."

Plum said, "I don't think there'll be a ladder. After all, this haystack was put here for cows."

Nancy said, "We could jerk off some of the hay and make ourselves little beds on the ground."

Plum said, "I'd rather sleep on the top. We don't know what's in this field. There might even be a bull."

Nancy said, "Oh, Plum, do you think so?" Her eyes were

wide and frightened, so Plum said, "No, I was just fooling." But just then, from the other side of the haystack there was a terrific snort. The girls clutched each other and Plum said, "Hold perfectly still. Maybe he won't be able to see us in the dark."

The snort came again louder and closer. The trembling little girls clutched each other tighter. Then suddenly against the pale moonlit sky appeared the frame of a fat plow horse.

"It's not a bull at all. It's a horse. A darling big old horse!" Plum almost shrieked in her relief. The horse lumbered toward them, Plum reached up and stroked his nose and he nuzzled her arm with his lips.

Nancy said, "Maybe he'll stand still and let us climb up on him and then we can get up on the haystack."

Plum said, "But how will we get up on him?"

Nancy said, "You climb up on my shoulders and I'll push you up on the horse and then you reach down and pull me up and then we will both climb up on the haystack."

Plum said, "It's a good idea if only Old Horse will stand still."

Nancy said, "Come on. He's right beside the haystack now. Here, I'll bend over. Now you climb on my shoulders."

Old Horse was very curious to know what the girls had in mind but he did stand still until they were both on his back. Then slowly and with great dignity he started galumphing across the field.

Plum called out, "Whoa, Old Horse. Whoa!"

The horse stopped, turned his head and looked at her.

Plum said, "I'll slide off and try to lead him over to the haystack again, Nancy. You hold on."

So Nancy clutched Old Horse's mane and Plum pushed his nose in the direction of the haystack and said, "Giddyup."

Old Horse walked back to the haystack but he went in underneath where the cows had been eating. Nancy had to lie down flat to avoid being buried in the haystack. In a muffled voice she called, "Plum, Plum, hurry and get him out of here."

Plum slapped Old Horse on the side and said, "Get out of there." So Old Horse did. He walked across the field again, Plum running after him calling, "Whoa! Whoa!" He finally stopped under a maple tree.

Plum said, "You'd better get off, Nancy. He'll never stand still."

So Nancy slid off and she and Plum ran back to the haystack to see if they couldn't figure out another way to climb up on it. Plum was pushing Nancy while she tried to climb the slippery hay, when Old Horse stuck his cold rubbery lips on the top of her head.

Plum said, "All right, Old Horse, I'll pat you if you'll help us. Now move over here close to the haystack and stand still."

Old Horse snorted knowingly and moved over. Nancy and Plum climbed up on his back again. Then with Plum calling, "Whoa!" constantly, he stood still while the two little girls pushed and pulled each other up to the top of the haystack. They called down their thanks to Old Horse and he snorted a little and moved into the hollowed out place.

The top of the haystack was rounded and quite scary until Nancy and Plum had jerked the hay aside and made themselves nice little deep nests. Little nests that smelled musty and were very stickery but felt like feather beds to the two tired little girls.

In no time at all Plum was dreaming about being a bareback rider in a circus and Nancy was dreaming about being adopted by a beautiful young mother and father.

The pale moon smiled on them and covered them with her soft, golden light. The night breezes peeked in at them and stroked their flushed faces with cool fingers. And Old Horse stamped his big feet and snorted to let them know that he was guarding them.

10

Looking for Work

MORNING CAME with a blare of noise and light. First a rooster crowed, "Cock-a-doodle-doo!" Some ducks said, "Quaaaaaa-ack, quaaaaaaack!" A cow bawled, "Moooooooooooooo." A dog barked, "Woo, woo, woooo." A sheep cried, "Baaaaaaaaaa-aaaaaaaaaaa!" A man's voice called, "So, boss. So, boss!" Some geese lifted their heads high on their stemlike necks and went, "Sssssssssssssssssssssssssssssss." A little bird sang, "Chick-a-dee-dee-dee-deee-deee." Old Horse galumphed to his feet and whinnied, "Wheeeeeeeeeeeeeee." Then a blazing sun leaped up from behind the hills and tossed a whole brimming bucket of sunlight over Nancy and Plum.

Nancy sat up and said, "Oh, doesn't that sunshine feel good? I got awfully cold in the night."

Plum said, "Sleeping in a haystack would be a lot more comfortable with blankets. Wow, I'm hungry."

Nancy said, "Oh, look over there. A farmhouse with smoke coming out of the chimney and there's a farmer carrying milk buckets."

Plum said, "I'm starving."

Nancy said, "We'd better hurry and get to town before Mrs. Monday finds we're gone."

Plum said, "She probably knows it already. It must be about six o'clock. Whee, watch me slide down the side of the haystack."

Nancy said, "You forgot your bundle of treasures. Here, catch. Now watch me."

She slid down. Then she and Plum patted Old Horse, ran across the field, climbed over the fence and started down the road.

On either side the wild roses, their pink dewy faces turned to the sun, tumbled over the fences, sprawled on the ground and filled the air with their pure summery smell. Freshly waxed buttercups crowded close to the road and great clumps of blue lupin and black-eyed Susans leaned forward to see over them. The billowing green fields wore white daisies like a light-falling snow and the distant hills were as purple as kings' robes. Meadowlarks threw back their heads and tossed lovely songs into the blue sky and like stars from rockets the notes hung there suspended for one breathless, exquisite moment. It was such a morning.

Nancy and Plum felt very frisky. They pranced in the

sunlight. Gathered bunches of the wild roses. Crushed tansy leaves. Colored their chins with the buttercups. Surprised fat bees in the lupin and told their fortunes with daisies.

Then the sun grew higher and hotter. Like the beam of a giant flashlight she focussed her blazing eye directly on them. The backs of their necks turned red, beads of sweat came out on their upper lips and the dust choked them. Not only that, but every time a car went by they either had to throw themselves down in the ditches beside the road or scramble behind bushes.

Plum threw a rock at a fence post and said, "We must have been walking for hours and hours and hours. Gosh, I'm hungry. Why don't we come to that old town?"

Nancy said, "The town's a long way from Mrs. Monday's but why don't we come to a stream? I'm so thirsty."

Plum said, "If we come to a stream I'm going swimming."

Nancy said, "Imagine lying in cool water with little leaves floating around and a big fat frog watching you."

Plum said, "People die of thirst, don't they?"

Nancy said, "In the desert they do. Their tongues swell up and they crawl across the sand calling, 'Water, water!' "

Plum said, "Hey, up ahead there is a grove of trees. Let's lie down in it and rest."

Nancy said, "Maybe we can find some wild strawberries."

Plum said, "Let's run. We can't be any hotter and we'll get there faster."

Nancy said, "All right, here we go."

When they reached the grove they found a funny old

grassy road branching off the main road and leading down a bank to a beautiful little stream with a deep brown pool almost hidden by willows.

"Oh, boy," Plum said as she kicked off her shoes, ripped off her jeans and shirt and jumped into the pool in her panties. "Oh, Nancy, hurry," she called. "It's sandy on the bottom and so cool."

Nancy jumped in and it was just as she had imagined it would be. Leaves and little sticks slowly whirled and drifted past, two fat green frogs peered out at them from the rushes and little shafts of sunlight pierced the tea-colored water and showed them their white feet and cloudy footsteps on the sandy bottom. They held their noses, opened their eyes under water and looked for periwinkles and minnows. They jumped off the bank and landed on the water, sitting down. They climbed on an old log and dove in belly-flop style. They floated on their backs and looked up at the sky through the trees. They found a tiny stream and made a dam. Plum caught a frog and named him Frank. Nancy started to gather rushes to weave a basket. Plum learned to whistle on a grass blade. If they hadn't been so very hungry they might have stayed there forever.

They were taking one last dive when suddenly a man's voice said, "How's the water?"

Plum looked at Nancy and they both looked scared.

The voice said, "Don't be frightened, girls. My name's Mr. Campbell and I own the haystack you slept in last night."

Plum said, "Did you know we slept in your haystack?"

Mr. Campbell said, "My wife saw you slide down and run

across the field this morning. She wanted me to ask you in for breakfast but I was out getting the cows and by the time she found me, you had disappeared."

Nancy said, "I hope you didn't mind our sleeping in your haystack."

Mr. Campbell said, "Glad to have you but how did you get up there?"

Plum said, "We used Old Horse, I mean your horse. We just called him Old Horse last night. He was awfully nice to us."

Mr. Campbell said, "Jerry's gentle as a kitten. He's too old to work much any more, so I just let him eat hay, get fat and enjoy himself."

Nancy said, "He stood still while we climbed on him. At first he wanted to take us for a ride but then Plum steered him back and made him stand by the haystack."

Mr. Campbell said, "Have you had a lot of experience with horses, Plum, is that right, Plum?"

Nancy said, "Her name's really Pamela but she called herself Plum when she was little."

Plum said, "I like horses and I'm not scared of them. Old To . . . I mean, a friend of mine used to let me help him with the horses and cows."

Mr. Campbell said, "Have you children had any breakfast?"

Plum said, "No, and we're starving."

Mr. Campbell said, "Well, I just pulled my wagon off the road to eat my sandwiches and I'd be glad to share them. Mrs. Campbell always fixes enough for an army."

Plum and Nancy said, "Oh, boy."

Mr. Campbell said, "I'll go up and spread the lunch out while you get dressed."

He turned and went up the road. They could hear him talking to his horses, so Plum and Nancy climbed up the bank, got clean, dry panties out of their bundles, put on their overalls and shirts, squeezed some of the water out of their hair, gathered up their treasures and old shoes and went up to join Mr. Campbell.

He was sitting on the grass beside his wagon, cracking a hard-boiled egg. On the grass around him were spread several red-and-white-checked napkins. On one was a stack of home-made bread-and-butter sandwiches. On another was a heap of cold fried chicken. On another were six smooth, brown, hard-boiled eggs. On another was a pile of sugar cookies as big as saucers. On another were three huge dill pickles and four bananas.

Plum looked at all the food and said, "Wow, Mr. Campbell, you must eat an awful lot."

Mr. Campbell laughed and said, "Well, actually I don't eat very much. But Mary Ann, that's Mrs. Campbell, always fixes enough food for ten men. She says that there's nothing she despises worse than a skimpy meal. Now help yourselves, children. There are two drumsticks, two wings and two second joints and that bread was baked yesterday."

Plum and Nancy were so hungry their hands shook as they reached for the fried chicken. They were on their third piece of chicken and fourth bread-and-butter sandwich when Mr.

Campbell said, "My gosh, I forgot the milk." He went to the wagon, reached under the seat and got a bundle of wet gunny sacking inside of which was a two-quart fruit jar of cool, rich milk. They drank right out of the jar, passing it back and forth and laughing at each other's creamy mustaches.

When finally they couldn't hold another bite, Mr. Campbell said, "Well, I guess I better get started if I'm going to get to town and back before midnight. Which way are you girls heading?"

Nancy said, "We're going to town to get a job."

Mr. Campbell said, "I'd be delighted to have you ride along with me. I had to take the wagon because I'm picking up a new cow in town, and though wagon riding is slow and kind of bumpy it is an awfully good way to see the country."

Plum said, "We'd certainly like to ride, if you don't care. We don't mind walking but our shoes are awfully worn out and the road's so dusty we can't always see the rocks."

Mr. Campbell said, "I'd rather wear no shoes than shoes with holes in 'em. If you're barefoot you know it and you walk carefully but if you have on shoes you forget about the hole and first thing you know you're stepping on a thistle."

After the girls had climbed up the high seat and settled themselves beside Mr. Campbell and after he had clucked to the horses and they had started down the road, he said, "What kind of work did you have in mind, Nancy?"

Nancy said, "Oh, washing dishes or baby sitting, something like that."

Plum said, "I'd rather milk cows or be a dog trainer, myself."

Mr. Campbell said, "Have you ever been to town before?"

Nancy and Plum said, "Oh, yes. We used to go every Library Day."

Mr. Campbell said, "Oh, so you live around here."

Plum said, "We used to."

Nancy said, "We might as well tell you, Mr. Campbell, we used to live at Mrs. Monday's Boarding Home and we're running away."

Mr. Campbell said, "Running away is kind of serious business. Are you sure it's the thing to do?"

So Nancy and Plum told him all about Mrs. Monday's. About Uncle John, the letter, the school program, the picnic, about Marybelle hiding Eunice's doll, even about Christmas and the empty box Plum found in the trunk room.

By the time they finished telling everything they were at the edge of town. Mr. Campbell said, "Well, Nancy and Plum, from what you've told me and from what I know about Mrs. Monday I'm on your side but I'd like to have Mary Ann's opinion on the matter. Now, I've got some business to attend to but I'll leave the wagon tied right here by this feed store. You go and see about your jobs, and I certainly wish you luck, however, if by some chance, you shouldn't find work you like or you need help, you come back here to the wagon and I'll be waiting."

Nancy and Plum thanked him, put on their shoes and socks, jumped out of the wagon and started up the street hand in hand. Mr. Campbell watched them until they rounded the corner by the drugstore and then he followed them, keeping out of sight by stepping into doorways and ducking down behind shrubs.

The first place where Nancy and Plum asked for a job was a large white house with a smooth green lawn. A woman with steel-rimmed glasses and a white uniform like a nurse's opened the door and said, "We don't allow solicitors."

Nancy said, "We're not solicitors. We want a job."

"Job?" the woman said, laughing in an unpleasant mocking way. "That's the silliest thing I ever heard of. Now go home to your mother and tell her to wash your dirty little faces." She slammed the door.

Nancy began to cry but Plum said, "Boy, I'm glad we don't work for her. She's crabbier than Mrs. Monday."

Nancy said, "I'm scared. What if we can't find a job?"

Plum said, "Then we'll just be like crickets and sleep in haystacks and eat berries and never have to work."

Nancy said, "Sleeping in haystacks is all right but we didn't get much to eat this morning until Mr. Campbell came along."

Plum said, "We had a good swim though. Here's a nice little house, let's go in here."

It was a small gray cottage with yellow roses climbing over the door and a shiny brass knocker, which Nancy timidly lifted and let fall once. Immediately one of the crisp white curtains at the front window was pushed aside and an old lady peered out at them. Nancy smiled at her, a tremulous smile, but Plum stared. After a while the old lady opened the door and asked them what they wanted. Plum said, "We would like work. Any kind of work."

The old lady smiled sweetly at them but said, "Land sakes, you are far too little to be looking for work. Now run along home."

She was nice but she thought they were just pretending and when Nancy tried to tell her that they really needed work, she only laughed and shut the door.

There was nobody home at the next house and at the next one a cross man told them to run along, his wife was sick. At the next house, a maid in a uniform told them that people who wanted work should go to the back door, and at the next house a little girl answered the door and stuck out her tongue.

They were just turning the corner to start on another street when they saw Mrs. Monday's black truck, cruising slowly along, Mrs. Monday, Old Tom and Marybelle in the front seat. Plum saw it first and before Nancy knew what it was all about she found herself lying flat on her face behind a hedge.

Angrily she said to Plum, "What's the matter with you? What's the idea of pushing me down?"

Carefully Plum parted the branches of the hedge and said, "Look."

Nancy looked and her face turned pale. "Oh, Plum," she whispered, "do you think they saw us?"

"I don't think so," Plum said. "We hadn't gotten around the corner yet and we were hidden by this hedge."

Nancy said, "Now we won't dare go up and down the streets looking for work."

Plum said, "Sure we will. We'll go down the alleys and knock at the back doors."

So all that long, disheartening afternoon they knocked at doors, asked for work and dodged Mrs. Monday and her truck.

They watched little children in bathing suits running through sprinklers, they saw fat babies kicking up their heels in baby carriages, they played peek-a-boo with babies in playpens, but nobody wanted a baby sitter. At least nobody seemed to want these small, shabby, dusty, barefooted baby sitters. Discouraged, they hid in a vacant lot, chewed the tender sweet ends of grass and wondered what to do.

Plum said, "Even if I have to go to jail I won't go back to Mrs. Monday's."

Nancy said, "I didn't think work would be so hard to find. I thought people needed help with their children."

Plum said, "I guess it's just that we're too little. Look, it must be dinnertime. See the fathers coming home. Say, I'll bet that means that Mrs. Monday has gone back to the Boarding Home."

Nancy said, "I ate so much lunch I never thought I'd be hungry again but I am, I'm awfully hungry."

Plum said, "I smelled so many good things when we were knocking at back doors that I got hungry a long time ago. Do you remember how good those chocolate cookies smelled in that house where the woman looked so tired and was so cross?"

Nancy said, "Best of all I liked the smell of fresh bread in that house that had the little boy who kicked us."

Plum said, "Do you suppose that Mr. Campbell really meant it when he said he'd wait for us?"

Nancy said, "Yes, I'm sure he meant it. He's a very kind man and I can tell by his eyes that he tells the truth."

Plum said, "Well, let's go and find him then, and see if we can sleep in his haystack again."

Nancy said, "Do you know where that feed store is?"

Plum said, "I'm not sure but I think it's over that way." She pointed north.

Nancy said, "Oh, no, Plum, you're wrong. I'm sure it's not that way. I think it is that way." She pointed south.

Plum said, "Well, as long as you think it is that way and I think it is that way, then let's go this way," and she pointed east.

Nancy said, "All right, we'll go five blocks this way and then we'll turn and go five blocks another way."

So they walked and they walked and they walked. They went this way and that way and the other way. Dinnertime passed and the fathers who had come home earlier stood in their shirt sleeves watering their lawns while the street rang with the cries of children playing catch and hide and seek. Occasionally mothers' voices called "Yohoo, Charlie, bedtime," screen doors slammed with a clack, front doors slammed with a dull boom. Cars drove by slowly, the tires making a gritty noise on the pavement.

Plum said, "I'm getting tired and I don't know where we are."

Nancy said, "I feel lonesome and all choky like I'm going to cry."

Plum said, "I think I'll just go up and knock on one of those doors and tell them we're lost."

Nancy said, "They'll send us back to Mrs. Monday's."

Plum said, "Well, there's no use our walking any more. We're not getting anywhere except loster."

Then away down the street they heard the clop, clop of horses' hooves and the creak of wagon wheels. Plum said, "Oh, Nancy, maybe that is Mr. Campbell. Maybe he's looking for us."

Nancy said, "Come on, let's run."

Sure enough it was Mr. Campbell. When he saw them he called out, "Thought you were never coming. I'm near starved. Hurry and climb in."

Nancy and Plum climbed in and then they both began to cry.

Mr. Campbell said, "Here, here, what's all this about?"

Plum said, "We couldn't find any work and we were lost."

Mr. Campbell said, "I followed you around most of the afternoon. Only lost track of you when I went to get the cow. What's the matter, don't the people in this town need any help?"

Nancy said, "They all said we're too little. One woman told us to go home and have our mother wash our dirty little faces."

Mr. Campbell said, "Well, I'll tell you, most children your size don't do much work."

Plum said, "But what will we do? We can't go back to Mrs. Monday's."

Mr. Campbell said, "Well, one thing you can do, Plum, is to drive for me. As soon as we get out of town here, I'd certainly appreciate a little help."

Plum wiped her eyes on her bundle of treasures and said, "Do you really mean it? May I drive?"

Mr. Campbell said, "Certainly I do. Now reach down there under the seat and you'll find a bag of hot roasted peanuts. One nice thing about fresh peanuts when you're driving in a wagon, they taste awful good, they don't spoil your appetite and you can throw the shells over your shoulder."

Nancy and Plum got out the peanuts and cracked and ate them ravenously in handfuls. Then Plum took the reins and Mr. Campbell ate peanuts.

After a while Plum said, "I forgot all about the cow." She turned around and looking behind her said, "Am I going too fast for you, old cowie?"

Mr. Campbell said, "I haven't named her yet. What do you suggest, Nancy?"

Nancy said, "Well, we could name her after Plum and me like we did Eunice's doll and call her Nanela?"

Mr. Campbell said, "I like that but do you think Eunice would like her doll to have the same name as a cow?"

Nancy said, "I suppose not. Maybe we'd better call her Wild Rose."

Mr. Campbell said, "I like that. Wild Rose is a very pretty name for a cow."

Plum said, "Oh, gosh, Mr. Campbell, there's a car coming. Will it scare the horses?"

He said, "No, Nellie and Herbert are used to cars but you children had better duck down under the seat just in case it might be Mrs. Monday."

Quickly the children got under the seat, Mr. Campbell yanked the old sacks that covered it down as far as he could and pulled the wagon over to the side of the road.

The car drew up beside them and stopped and Mrs. Monday's voice called out, "Is that you, Mr. Campbell?"

Mr. Campbell said, "Sure is, Mrs. Monday."

Mrs. Monday said, "Have you seen two little girls walking along the road?"

Mr. Campbell said, "Have not. What's the matter, have you lost some?"

Mrs. Monday said, "Two of my boarders, Nancy and Pamela Remson, both absolutely incorrigible children, have run away and I'm almost frantic with worry."

Mr. Campbell said, "I'm sure sorry, Mrs. Monday. Well, I gotta be getting along home."

Mrs. Monday said, "If the children should come to your farm and ask for food or shelter, tie them up and call me on the telephone."

Mr. Campbell said, "Tie them up?"

Mrs. Monday said, "Yes, tie them up. They are the kind of children who kick and bite if they can't have their own way."

Mr. Campbell said, "I'll watch out for them, Mrs. Monday. Good-night."

Mrs. Monday and Old Tom drove off in the direction of town and the girls climbed out from under the seat. They were trembling.

Mr. Campbell said, "Gosh, I didn't know you two were so dangerous. Do you really bite and kick?"

Plum said, "Of course we don't."

Nancy said, "If she ever catches us I'll bet she never gives us anything to eat again."

Mr. Campbell said, "Oh, come now. She wouldn't starve you."

Nancy said, "She always takes our food away for punishment."

Plum said, "Really having to eat her awful food is the worst punishment, but she was always making us go to bed without any supper. Old Tom says that's why we're so little and skinny."

Mr. Campbell said, "Well, I'm not trying to punish you and yet here I am keeping you from supper. I'll bet Mary Ann's almost wild and I'll bet she's got enough food ready to feed every boarder at Mrs. Monday's."

Plum said, "What do you think she might have?"

Mr. Campbell said, "Well, let's see, this is Saturday. That means a big stone crock of baked beans, all molassesy and filled with chunks of salt pork. Then there will be brown bread, sliced tomato and cucumber salad, country sausage cakes, apple pie and cheese. Milk and coffee, of course."

Nancy said, "Do you suppose she will mind if you bring us home for supper?"

Mr. Campbell said, "Well, I might as well confess that she

sent me after you today. She said, 'Angus Campbell, if you come home tonight without finding out about those two little girls, I'll be madder than a wet hen.' "

Plum said, "How far are we from your farm?"

Mr. Campbell said, "Around the next bend and turn to your left. Did the peanuts hurt your appetite any?"

Nancy and Plum said, "No!" so loudly that Mr. Campbell laughed.

Then they went around the bend and turned to the left and there was Mrs. Campbell on the back porch holding a lantern. She said, "Well, my goodness, I thought you were never coming. I've had the table set for three solid hours."

Mr. Campbell said, "Mary Ann, I brought Nancy and Plum Remson home to supper."

Mrs. Campbell said, "Nancy and Plum? Is that what you said?"

Plum said, "My name's really Pamela but I called myself Plum when I was little."

Mrs. Campbell said, "Well, hop down and come right in. You must be starved. Angus, hurry and put the team away and unload that cow. I've already done the milking and fed the chickens."

As Nancy and Plum climbed down from the wagon, Mrs. Campbell said, "Where are your shoes and stockings?"

Plum said, "Our shoes are in the wagon but they have such big holes in them we might as well be barefoot."

Mrs. Campbell said, "Well, I'll put some newspapers

down—I just scrubbed my kitchen floor." She spread a newspaper path between the kitchen door and the big range in the corner of the kitchen and directed Nancy and Plum to stay on these papers. Gingerly on careful tiptoe they walked across the kitchen, which was delightfully cozy and smelled tantalizingly of the baked beans and apple pie.

Mrs. Campbell told them to sit on the woodbox. Then she got a basin of warm water and vigorously scrubbed their faces, hands and dirty little feet. "Now," she said as she scrubbed Nancy's face with a rough, lavender-scented towel, "I can see what you look like. Well, I never was able to make a choice between red and yellow hair, yours are my favorite kind of eyes, you look smart and I am partial to little girls. Now sit up there at the table and let's start putting a little meat on those bones."

Shyly Nancy and Plum sat down at the table while Mrs. Campbell heaped pink-flowered plates with baked beans, sausage cakes and salad, passed a steaming plate of brown bread, cut them off generous pieces of the pat of new butter and handed them big mugs of ice-cold milk.

While she was serving them, Mr. Campbell came in, washed quickly and sat down. Then Plum and Nancy bowed their heads and said:

"God is great and God is good,
And we thank Him for this food.
By His hand may we be led,
Give us Lord our daily bread."

Mrs. Campbell said, "I learned the same grace when I was a little girl, Plum. Did Mrs. Monday teach you that?"

Nancy said, "No, our mother taught us that. Almost every child at Mrs. Monday's says a different grace. She had us take turns."

Mrs. Campbell said, "I'm surprised. She came by here today and wanted to know if two little girls had been to the house to ask for food and shelter. I told her no and that was the truth because you hadn't. I could have told her that I saw two little girls climbing down out of our old haystack this morning but I just didn't want to. There is something about that woman that riles me."

Mr. Campbell said, "As soon as you're through eating, Nancy and Plum, tell Mrs. Campbell all about Mrs. Monday, Uncle John and Marybelle."

And they did. They told her while they were helping her clear the table and wash the dishes. She kept saying, "That woman!" and slapping the dishmop against the plates.

When all the dishes had been dried and put away, the oil-cloth tablecloth had been wiped with a damp cloth, the stove had been whisked off with a turkey feather, the immaculate floor had been swept free of crumbs, the pots of red geraniums on the window sill had been given a drink of water, the old orange cat had been given a saucer of milk behind the stove and the collie dog had been fed, Nancy and Plum said, "Now if you don't mind, we'll go down to the haystack."

Mrs. Campbell said, "You'll do no such thing. I've got three spare bedrooms in this house and nobody to sleep in them."

Nancy and Plum said, "But we haven't any nightgowns."

Mrs. Campbell said, "I've already thought of that. You can wear Angus's nightshirts."

Nancy and Plum said, "Are you sure we won't be any trouble?"

Mrs. Campbell said, "Trouble? My goodness, when were children any trouble? Now scoot upstairs before you fall asleep right in your tracks."

Mrs. Campbell held the lamp and led the way up the stairs, down a hallway carpeted in bright rag runners and into a large square room at the end of the hall. Setting the lamp in a holder by the door, she told the girls to get undressed, opened up a drawer in the high chiffonier and handed them each a blue-and-white-checked flannel nightshirt. When they knelt to say their prayers the nightshirts dragged on the floor and the sleeves hung to their knees but Plum said, "They are certainly warmer and softer than hay."

The bed, a huge four-poster with a canopy, was so high that they had to use a little ladder to climb into it and when they got in they sank almost out of sight.

Mrs. Campbell laughed and said, "How do you like my grandmother's feather bed?"

Nancy said, "I feel like I'm on a cloud."

Plum said, "This is the way I have always imagined beds. All floaty and smelling like lavender."

Mrs. Campbell pushed aside the white ruffled curtains, opened the windows wide, then came over to the bed, leaned down and kissed each of them good-night. Nancy and Plum said good-night and their eyes above the patchwork quilt were like stars.

After Mrs. Campbell had gone with the lamp, Nancy said, "Doesn't Mrs. Campbell smell good. Like cinnamon and fresh bread."

Plum said, "She's beautiful."

Nancy said, "And Mr. Campbell is very handsome."

Of course they weren't at all. Mrs. Campbell was round and cozy with sparkling brown eyes, curly brown hair and rosy cheeks but she wasn't beautiful. Mr. Campbell was tall and thin with merry blue eyes and stiff sandy hair but he wasn't handsome. They were good and kind however, and oftentimes goodness and kindness cast a glow over people that passes very well for beauty.

11

Back to Mrs. Monday's

THE NEXT MORNING, Nancy and Plum were waked up by the orange cat, Penny, lying between them, purring with a noise like a bee on a screen. Plum reached over and scratched her behind the ears, and Penny put out a soft paw and touched Plum's cheek.

Then Nancy felt something cold and wet against her arm. She turned over to find Sandy, the collie, his paws on the bed, his nose between his paws, his brown eyes pleading for play. Nancy scratched Sandy behind the ears and said, "I'll bet it's awfully late. Oh, what a comfortable bed!"

Plum said, "I don't think I'll ever get up."

A voice from the doorway said, "Well, lazybones, are you

going to sleep all day? I was counting on a little help with the milking."

Plum said, "Oh, Mr. Campbell, I forgot about getting up early to milk. I suppose you're all through."

He said, "I'm all through for this morning, even fed the calves, but you can help me tonight and if you get right up, you can gather the eggs."

"Oh, boy," Plum said, leaping out of bed. In her enthusiasm she forgot about the long nightshirt and the high bed and landed in a heap like a tangled bundle of laundry. Mr. Campbell and Nancy laughed, Sandy barked and Penny looked disgusted.

Mr. Campbell said, "Mrs. Campbell has waffles and ham all ready for anybody that's interested," and went out.

"Last one dressed is a fleabeetle," Plum said, yanking on her clothes.

Carefully Nancy climbed out of bed and began putting on her clothes. She said, "I don't care if you do beat me this morning, Plum, I feel slow and ladylike."

When they were both dressed, had combed and braided their hair, turned back the bed, hung the nightshirts in the closet and closed the bedroom door, they went down to the kitchen.

Mrs. Campbell was standing at the stove taking sizzling pieces of thick pink ham out of an iron skillet and putting them on a brown earthenware platter. She smiled at them and said, "Good-morning, good-morning. Come and give me a big hug and a kiss."

The girls walked to her shyly and she enveloped them in a strong, comforting, waffly smelling hug, gave them each a kiss and said, "The bathroom's right off that hall in there. Go in and splash a little cold water on your faces and hurry because I have a waffle all ready for you."

Plum said, "Everything in this house smells awfully good."

Mrs. Campbell said, "When you're hungry there's no perfume like the smell of frying ham. Now scat."

Nancy said, "As soon as I wash, I'll set the table for you."

Mrs. Campbell said, "Oh, goodness, honey, I've had the breakfast table set for an hour."

After splashing icy water on their faces and rubbing them fiery red with one of the rough sweet-smelling towels, they came in and took their places at the big kitchen table. This morning the table wore a bright red-and-white-checked cloth and a pot of red geraniums. Mrs. Campbell handed the girls their plates, each with a slice of ham and a half of a crisp tan waffle. Nancy said, "We've seen pictures of waffles in magazines but we've never tasted them before."

Mrs. Campbell said, "Well, bless your hearts. What did that woman give you for breakfast?"

"Prunes and oatmeal," Nancy said.

"Yes," Plum said, "prunes that were all skin and pits and burnt oatmeal."

Mrs. Campbell said, "Mrs. Monday doesn't have the look of a good cook about her."

Plum said, "Katie did the cooking but Mrs. Monday told her what to cook for us boarders. Anyway, she and Marybelle had different food. They had waffles sometimes."

Mrs. Campbell said, "Different food?"

Plum said, "Yep, they sat at a little table all by themselves. Sometimes they had chicken pies. Little bubbly ones with golden crusts."

Mrs. Campbell said, "Would you like to have a chicken pie for dinner?"

Plum said, "Oh, more than anything. I've longed for chicken pie so much that sometimes I dream about it, then I wake up in the morning ashamed because I'm so greedy."

Mrs. Campbell said, "I don't think it's greedy to dream about good food but I certainly think it's greedy to serve one kind of food to your boarders and eat another, better kind yourself."

Nancy said, "Do you know something, Mrs. Campbell, I've always wanted to learn to cook. Would you let me watch you make the chicken pie? I mean stand close so I can see everything."

Mrs. Campbell said, "What's better, I'll let you make it yourself."

Nancy said, "Oh, but I wouldn't know how."

"No time like the present to learn," Mrs. Campbell said, leaning down and kissing the top of Nancy's head as she put another waffle on her plate.

Plum said, "Mr. Campbell said that I could gather the eggs."

Mrs. Campbell said, "And he meant it, too, but you'd better eat another waffle so you'll have enough strength to carry the basket. We don't want any little weak arms dropping all our eggs and breaking them."

Plum said, "Even if I wasn't going to gather the eggs I'd eat another waffle. Next to chicken pie I guess I like waffles best of anything."

Mrs. Campbell said, "Who braided your hair so nice and neat?"

Plum and Nancy said, "We braid each other's."

Nancy said, "Notice how straight we get our parts." She bent her head so Mrs. Campbell could see. "That's one of the first things you learn at Mrs. Monday's. Straight parts and tight, even braids."

Plum said, through a mouth full of waffle and maple syrup, "When we first went there and were very little, she used to braid our hair herself and she braided it so tight we couldn't close our eyes."

Nancy said, "She even makes children with curly hair wear pigtails."

Mrs. Campbell said, "Well, Marybelle Whistle certainly has a head loaded with corkscrews."

Both children giggled at this description and Plum told Mrs. Campbell how she used to call Marybelle Woodenhead with shaving curls.

Mrs. Campbell said, "I've always wondered why Marybelle lives with her aunt. She has parents, hasn't she?"

Nancy said, "Oh, yes, she's got a mother and father but her mother has sick headaches."

Plum said, "Probably got them from looking at Marybelle."

Mrs. Campbell said, "Well, now we can't sit around here talking all day. Plum, you go down and gather your eggs and tell Mr. Campbell that we're going to have chicken pie for dinner and I need a nice fat hen. Also tell him I want some peas and carrots, a head of lettuce and some radishes and onions from the garden."

Plum said, "Don't you want me to help you with the dishes?"

Mrs. Campbell said, "My goodness, no, honey, you go help Mr. Campbell and Nancy will help me."

Plum jumped up and was just skipping out the door when Mrs. Campbell called her back. "Just a minute, Plum," she said. "Let me take a look at those shoes."

Plum slipped off her shoes and handed them to her and when Mrs. Campbell turned them over and saw the huge holes she said, "Tsk, tsk," and with the kitchen shears and some heavy cardboard, set about making insoles. When they were finished, Plum slipped them on, said, "Wow! Just like new shoes," thanked Mrs. Campbell and went racing off to the barn.

Mrs. Campbell said to Nancy, "Now let me have yours, honey. I fixed Plum's first because it's very dangerous to be around the barns in bare feet."

Nancy said, "Do new shoes cost very much?"

Mrs. Campbell said, "Not very much."

Nancy said, "Well, when I get a job and earn some money, that's the first thing I'm going to buy."

Mrs. Campbell said, "Speaking of jobs, we'd better get the dishes done or we'll never get at that chicken pie."

It was while Mrs. Campbell and Nancy were upstairs making the beds that Old Tom drove into the yard. He drove the black truck right up by the back porch, got out and knocked on the door. Nancy ran into a closet and hid behind the clothes but Mrs. Campbell said, "Come on, Nancy, hiding won't do any good at all. Let's go down and see what he has to say."

Old Tom said, "She doesn't know Nancy and Plum are here, Mrs. Campbell, but I knew because I told them to sleep in your haystack. What I stopped in to tell you is that Mrs. Monday has called their Uncle John and he is on his way out. Shall I have him come up here?"

Mrs. Campbell said, "By all means. I'd like to talk to him."

Nancy put her arms around Mrs. Campbell, buried her head in her apron and said, "No, please don't. We'll have to go back to Mrs. Monday's. Please don't."

Mrs. Campbell patted her head and said, "Don't worry, honey, I'll watch out for you."

Mr. Campbell and Plum came up from the barn carrying the fat red hen. Mr. Campbell said, "What is it, Tom?"

Old Tom said, "Mrs. Monday doesn't know the girls are here but she has called their Uncle John and I want to know if I should bring him up here."

Mr. Campbell said, "Of course, I want to talk to him."

178

Plum threw her arms around Mr. Campbell's legs, buried her face in his overalls and cried, "No, please, don't. He'll send us back to Mrs. Monday's. Please don't send us back to Mrs. Monday's."

Mr. Campbell patted her head and said, "Don't you worry, honey, I'll take care of you."

Old Tom rubbed his forehead and said, "Nancy and Plum, I'm only trying to help you. This will be your chance to talk to your uncle and tell him about Mrs. Monday."

Mrs. Campbell said, "If he has the gumption of a rabbit he'll see how skinny and undersized they are."

Plum said, "And how worn out our shoes are."

Old Tom said, "How was that haystack anyway, girls?"

Nancy wiped her eyes on Mrs. Campbell's apron and said, "Oh, it was wonderful, Tom. Like sleeping on a cloud."

Plum said, "A cloud made of splinters."

Mrs. Campbell said, "What time do you think their uncle will get here?"

Old Tom said, "Well, she just got hold of him and Central City's a long way off."

Plum said, "Come on, Uncle Angus, let's hurry and pick that chicken. If I have to go back to Mrs. Monday's I'm going to eat that chicken pie first."

Nancy said, "Uncle Angus?"

Plum said, "Yes, he asked me to call him that, didn't you, Uncle Angus?"

Mr. Campbell said, "Certainly did. Wish you'd call me Uncle Angus, too, Nancy."

Mrs. Campbell said, "And I'm Aunt Mary Ann from now on."

Plum said, "I think I'll call Uncle John Mr. Remson."

Mrs. Campbell said, "Now listen. This is what I think we'd better do. We'll all go about our business and enjoy ourselves as much as possible. Then when Uncle John and Mrs. Monday get here we'll talk things over in a nice sensible way, without getting angry. I'm sure everything will turn out for the best."

Plum said, "What if Mrs. Monday lies? She always does, you know."

Mr. Campbell said, "We'll handle that when the time comes. Now come on and let's see how fast you can get the feathers off that chicken."

The chicken pie was perfection. Little bubbles of gravy came up through the pricks on the golden flaky crust. The inside was all big pieces of tender chicken, sweet new peas, tiny whole carrots, little white onions and rich fragrant gravy.

Plum took her first bite and said, "Now I'm madder than I ever was at Mrs. Monday and Marybelle."

Mr. Campbell took his first bite and said, "I hate to say this, Nancy, but you're a better cook than Mary Ann."

Mrs. Campbell said, "Good cooks are born that way, I always say, and Nancy is certainly one of the best."

Nancy was so happy and proud she glistened.

It was unfortunate that just at this moment Uncle John, Marybelle and Mrs. Monday should have arrived.

With a moan Plum looked out the window, saw Uncle

John's big car and began stuffing the chicken pie in her mouth. It was scalding hot and after each bite she had to gulp a swallow of ice-cold milk.

Nancy said, "Plum, you're being disgusting."

Plum said, "I dod care. Nobody's goig to keep me frob eatig this chicked pie."

Mr. Campbell said, "That's right, Plum, now is no time to stand on ceremony. Choke it down before they get here."

Mrs. Campbell said, "I'll heat up what's left and you can have it for supper, Plum."

Nancy pushed her plate away and said, "I feel kind of sick."

Mrs. Campbell kissed her cheek and said, "I know just how you feel, honey, but don't you worry. Everything's going to be all right."

Uncle John was very cool to Nancy and Plum and Mrs. Monday didn't speak to them at all. Marybelle hissed at Plum, "Boy, you're going to get it," and Plum said, "So are you," and stamped on her toe.

Marybelle gave a shriek and said, "Aunty Marybelle, Plum stepped on my toe."

Plum said, "I'm terribly sorry, Mrs. Monday, I must not have been looking where I was going."

Mr. Campbell winked at Plum as they all filed into the parlor.

When they were seated, Uncle John said, "Nancy and Pamela, I was very distressed to hear of your running away. Most inconsiderate of you. You have caused Mrs. Monday

181

worry and you have certainly upset me. I trust such a thing will never happen again."

Plum said, "It certainly won't because we will never go back to Mrs. Monday's."

Uncle John said, "You will go back to Mrs. Monday's."

Nancy said, "But, Uncle John, you can't send us back there! You don't know how awful she treats us."

Uncle John said, "All children must have discipline. You know that, Nancy. Discipline is part of training and I am paying Mrs. Monday to train you."

Plum said, "Is taking away our supper and making us wear shoes with holes in them training?" She held up her foot for Uncle John to see.

He looked at the hole and turned to Mrs. Monday.

She laughed and said, "I told you, Mr. Remson, that Nancy and Plum chose special little costumes for this act they are putting on. You saw their lovely clothes, and their many pairs of new shoes."

Plum said, "That's not true, Mrs. Monday. We don't have any lovely clothes or new shoes and you know it."

Uncle John said, "Pamela, I will not tolerate such impudence. With my own eyes I saw yours and Nancy's entire, very complete wardrobes. Now I am tired of this nonsense. Get in the car and we will go!"

Mr. Campbell said, "Mr. Remson, are you sure of your facts?"

Uncle John said, "I certainly am."

Mr. Campbell said, "Has it occurred to you that well-cared-for children are not as thin and undersized as Nancy and Plum?"

Mrs. Monday said, "Nancy and Pamela are extremely spoiled children, Mr. Campbell. They like to eat nothing but sweets, which accounts for their slight bodies."

Uncle John said, "Their mother was also small and very slender. Size is hereditary."

Nancy said, "Uncle John, did you look at the other boarders at Mrs. Monday's? They are all little and skinny, too."

Uncle John waved his hand in the direction of fat Marybelle and said, "That is an obvious untruth, Nancy. Now I have had quite enough of this arguing. Mr. and Mrs. Campbell, I will send you a check for your trouble."

Mrs. Campbell, her cheeks flaming and her eyes flashing, said, "We don't want anything from you, Mr. Remson. Nancy and Plum were no trouble."

Mr. Campbell said, "You must be very anxious to be rid of your nieces, Mr. Remson."

Uncle John said, "I know very little about children but I have spared no expense in caring for Nancy and Pamela. It is my opinion that Mrs. Monday is doing everything in her power to give them a good, normal home."

Plum, who was crying, said, "If good, normal homes were like Mrs. Monday's every child in the world would run away."

Mr. Remson said, "Pamela, you are not only ungrateful but very rude. Apologize to Mrs. Monday."

Plum said, "I won't apologize to Mrs. Monday and the next time I run away I'm going to Africa."

Mrs. Monday turned to Uncle John and said, "You see, Mr. Remson, I have a real problem in these children."

Nancy, who was also crying, her head buried in Mrs. Campbell's lap, looked up and said, "Mrs. Monday, you don't tell the truth and your heart is going to turn pure black."

Plum said, "What heart?"

Uncle John said, "I've had enough of this and I must get back to the city. Nancy and Pamela, go out to the car. You will sit in front with the driver."

Nancy and Plum threw their arms around Mrs. Campbell and said, "Good-bye, Aunt Mary Ann."

Mrs. Campbell patted them and whispered, "Don't you worry. We'll work this out some way. Go along with them quietly now and remember we'll help you."

Nancy said, "You keep our treasures, Aunt Mary Ann."

Plum said, "And save my chicken pie for me."

Then they hugged Mr. Campbell and he patted them and whispered, "Don't worry, we're smarter than Mrs. Monday. We'll figure something out."

Plum wailed, "But I never got to milk the cow."

Mr. Campbell said, "You will, Plum. Soon, too."

After they were settled in the car and were driving along toward the Boarding Home, Nancy said to Plum, "Remember yesterday morning how beautiful we thought this road was?"

Plum said, "It looks ugly and dreary now."

And it did, too. Dark clouds had gathered and hung low, their black shadows lying on the valley like shrouds. The wild roses had hidden their heads, the buttercups had closed up tight and even the black-eyed Susans turned their faces away as the long black car went past. By the time they reached the Boarding Home, a wind had come up, big splatty drops of rain were falling and the day had turned to dusk.

As they got out of the car, Uncle John said, "I understand you won the spelling match at school, Pamela."

Plum did not answer.

Mrs. Monday said, "Sulking. Another one of their bad habits."

Uncle John said, "Did the new dress I sent you fit all right, Nancy?"

Nancy said, "We have never gotten anything from you, Uncle John. Not even a letter."

Mrs. Monday said, "Nancy, it is wicked to tell falsehoods to your uncle. Now, my dear, dear Mr. Remson, I know how eager you are to get back to the city, so we won't take up any more of your time."

Uncle John said, "Good-bye, Nancy and Pamela."

Nancy and Plum turned and looked at him. Their eyes were as cold as frost and they said not one word as they turned and went up the steps of the Boarding Home.

Mrs. Monday shook hands with Uncle John and then hurried through the rain and into the house. Uncle John's car drove off, its red taillights in the gloom like two evil eyes.

Nancy and Plum were waiting for Mrs. Monday in the hall. She said, "Come along with me. I have moved you. I'll show you to your new room."

She took them to the third floor and down the hall to the trunk room.

"I had Tom move all the trunks and boxes to the attic," she said. "From now on this will be your room and you will be locked in." There was a large new lock on the door. Mrs. Monday unlocked it with a little key she wore fastened to a slender silver necklace.

The trunk room was very dark and their little iron bed against the brown wall looked like a prison cot.

Mrs. Monday said, "Because of the sloping ceiling, your bureau wouldn't fit in here, so you will use that box." She pointed to a plain wooden box in which Nancy and Plum's meager collection of clothing had been dumped carelessly.

She said, "I think it would be a good idea for you to stay up here and think about what naughty and inconsiderate little girls you have been."

Nancy and Plum just looked at her. She went out, closing and locking the door after her.

Nancy walked over and stood by the window. A jagged flash of lightning pierced a black cloud like a flaming dart. Big fat clouds bumped into each other and grumbled menacingly. The rain on the roof sounded like hundreds of woodpeckers. Raindrops hit against the window and rolled down the glass like tears. Nancy watched them and as she watched matching tears rolled out of her eyes and down her cheeks.

186

There was another grumble from the clouds, this time much louder. Lightning lit up the little room.

Plum said, "You don't scare me, you old lightning bolts. Nothing scares me any more." Then she threw herself down on the bed face down, and Nancy could hear her sobbing even above the whining wind, the thrumming rain and the growling thunder.

12

Chicken Pie and New Shoes

BACK AT THE FARM, Mr. Campbell hurried around feeding the animals and getting them under shelter. He was so angry that he slammed doors, shot the bolts and banged water buckets and feed pails until it sounded like the Fourth of July.

Nellie and Herbert, the horses, put their ears forward and looked at him in amazement. Wild Rose and Susie, the cows, got scared, switched their tails and tried to jerk their heads out of their stanchions. The chickens went, "Waaaak, waaaak, waaaak!" and flew straight up in the air. The geese said, "Hisssssssssssssssss," and ran with their heads forward and their wings up like fat ladies holding up their skirts and running to get out of the rain. Only the pigs didn't care. "Slurp, slurp, gulp," they said, up to their eyes in their food and not

188

caring whether Mr. Campbell shot their dinner at them out of a cannon or hit them on the head with it, just so there was plenty.

In the house, Mrs. Campbell slammed the ice-box door, banged the lids on the stove, thumped the churn, whacked the butter into pats with the paddle and said to herself, "That woman. That awful woman!"

That night after supper as she took out the quilt she was piecing, she said, "Angus, we have to do something. Right now!" She bit off a piece of thread angrily.

Mr. Campbell lit his pipe, blew a big thick smoke ring and said, "I was so furious after they left I could barely control myself, then after I'd worked out my anger on the feed buckets and a few doors I got to thinking. What we have to do, Mary Ann, is to prove that Mrs. Monday is not telling the truth. That she doesn't give her little boarders good or kind care. That she has deliberately deceived Uncle John. But *how?*"

Mrs. Campbell said, "Well, how?"

Mr. Campbell said, "I haven't figured it out yet."

Mrs. Campbell said, "Well, I have. Tomorrow morning, right after breakfast, I'm going into town to see Miss Appleby. She knows Nancy and Plum and she knows how Mrs. Monday used to keep them home from the library for punishment. Then I'm going to see Miss Waverly and I'm going to ask them both to go to Central City and see Uncle John."

Mr. Campbell said, "If and when we are able to convince Uncle John that Mrs. Monday is not fit to take care of Nancy and Plum, what then?"

189

"Why," said Mrs. Campbell, "they are coming here to live, of course."

Mr. Campbell smiled and said, "I hoped you'd say that. I used to dream of having a little girl and in my dreams she was always just like Plum."

Mrs. Campbell said, "And I've always dreamed of having a little girl and in my dreams she was just like Nancy."

Mr. Campbell said, "Of course, I love Nancy too, but Plum is so good with animals and she has so much spirit."

Mrs. Campbell said, "Of course, I love Plum too, but Nancy is so little girly, so gentle and dreamy."

Mr. Campbell said, "We couldn't be better satisfied if we'd had them ourselves."

Mrs. Campbell said, "They're heaven sent, that's what." She stopped her sewing and stroked the cat and her eyes were brimming with tears.

The next morning early, Mr. and Mrs. Campbell got in their old blue sedan and headed for town. The storm had settled the dust and the whole countryside was clean and fresh and sweet smelling from the rain.

When they got to town, they drove straight to the library. Miss Appleby was very glad to see them and started to tell Mrs. Campbell about two very good new novels that had come in but Mrs. Campbell cut her short. She said, "Miss Appleby, we've got to have your help and we've got to have it today. Can you get someone to take your place?"

"Certainly," said Miss Appleby. "Miss Warren will substitute for me any time. But what in the world is the matter?"

Mr. and Mrs. Campbell told her about Nancy and Plum running away, about their coming to their house, about Uncle John and Mrs. Monday. Before they had half finished, Miss Appleby said, "Don't tell me any more. I'm already so mad I'm about to burst."

Mrs. Campbell said, "Well, what I want you to do is to get hold of Miss Waverly and the two of you go into Central City and see Mr. Remson and tell him the truth. Make him listen. Make him realize that Mrs. Monday is deceiving him. Tell him about Nancy and Plum's school clothes. Tell him about the program and the holes in Plum's shoes and Nancy having to wear a tree costume. Tell him how hard they have to work. Tell him that they spent last Christmas in a barn all alone. Tell him that they have never had enough to eat since they went there. Tell him how Plum mailed Nancy's letter. Tell him that it might be a good idea if he asked Nancy and Plum to describe the wardrobes of clothes they are supposed to have and to list the gifts he has sent them and that Mrs. Monday swears they have received."

Miss Appleby said, "Oh, Mary Ann, what if Miss Waverly isn't here? She was supposed to visit her brother in Florida and I'm afraid she has already left."

Mrs. Campbell said, "Call her on the telephone, right now, and see."

Miss Appleby did and Mrs. Wentil said that Miss Waverly had just that minute gone but she would try to catch her. She said that she would call back.

While they waited for the call, Miss Appleby sent

191

Mr. Campbell over to get Miss Warren, then she and Mrs. Campbell went on with their plans.

Miss Appleby said, "Imagine those two poor little things having to sit there while that unscrupulous woman told their uncle they were sulky and ate nothing but sweets."

Mrs. Campbell said, "I was tickled to death when Nancy told Mrs. Monday she didn't tell the truth and her heart would turn black and Plum said, 'What heart?' "

Miss Appleby said, "What makes me so furious is that two such unusually brilliant and sensitive children should be in the care of such a stupid and insensitive woman."

Mrs. Campbell said, "Plum told her uncle that she wouldn't stay at Mrs. Monday's and the next time she ran away it would be to Africa."

Miss Appleby said, "And for Mr. Remson to believe that awful Mrs. Monday. Of course, he couldn't care anything at all about those children or he would never have put them in Mrs. Monday's in the first place. One look at that spiked fence would have been enough for me."

Then Mr. Campbell and Miss Warren came in and the phone rang and it was Miss Waverly.

Miss Appleby said, "Peggy Waverly, get in your car and come over here to the library right away. It's terribly important and too long to discuss on the phone."

Miss Waverly said, "But I'm all packed to leave for Florida."

And Miss Appleby said, "This is right on your way and it's an opportunity you wouldn't miss for the world."

She hung up the phone, turned to the Campbells and said, "Now you run along home and don't worry. Everything will be all right and Nancy and Plum won't have to stay at Mrs. Monday's. You'd better go home and bake a big chicken pie, Mary Ann, because I have a hunch Peggy, Mr. Remson, Nancy and Plum and I will all be there for supper."

Mrs. Campbell took out her handkerchief, dabbed at the corners of her eyes and said, "I couldn't ever make a chicken pie as good as the one Nancy made."

Miss Appleby said, "I'm glad to know that Nancy's such a good cook, but I'll take a chance on supper at your house, any day."

When they got in the car, Mrs. Campbell said, "I want to stop at Gatsby's department store a minute. Those children can't sleep in your nightshirts forever and I'm going to get them each a pair of shoes."

"How can you get them shoes without trying them on?" Mr. Campbell asked.

"This way," Mrs. Campbell said, reaching in her purse and taking out the two cardboard insoles. "I drew around their bare feet to make these," she said. "And I'm going to get them those pretty colored tennis shoes. Bright red for Plum and blue for Nancy. I'm going to buy them some new blue jeans and T-shirts, too," she added defiantly.

Mr. Campbell said, "Anything you get Nancy and Plum is all right with me. Got enough money?"

"Plenty," said Mrs. Campbell through set lips.

"Well then," said Mr. Campbell, "I'll pick you up here in about half an hour."

When Mr. Campbell stopped for Mrs. Campbell, she was laden with packages and he sheepishly admitted that he had done a little shopping, too.

He said, "I looked in those bundles of 'treasures' as they called them, and, Mary Ann, those kids don't have anything. A string of broken beads, a dried june bug, a snake's skin and some rocks full of fool's gold is all Plum had."

Mrs. Campbell said, "And Nancy had a little china doll with the head off, some paper dolls cut out of a magazine and a little locket with a broken chain."

Mr. Campbell said, "Well, I bought Plum a pocketknife. A very good one with two blades, a screw driver, can opener, nail file, scissors and an awl in it."

Mrs. Campbell said, "A knife, Angus? I certainly hope she won't hurt herself."

Mr. Campbell said, "Plum won't hurt herself. You don't need to worry about her."

"What did you get Nancy?" Mrs. Campbell asked.

"A little sewing box," Mr. Campbell said. "It's green leather and it has scissors, a thimble, needles, pins, a tape measure and little spools of different colored thread. Do you think she'll like that?"

"Well, I should say so," Mrs. Campbell said, "I'd like one myself."

They both laughed. Then Mrs. Campbell said, "I bought

them pajamas, bedroom slippers, tennis shoes, blue jeans and T-shirts."

Mr. Campbell said, "I got a couple of other little things, too. Straw farmer hats and some bubble bath."

"Oh, Angus," Mrs. Campbell said. "Bubble bath! I know they'll love that."

By five o'clock, Mrs. Campbell had the chicken pie in baking, the table set, the salad made and she was frosting a huge coconut cake. Mr. Campbell had the barn swept, the milk-room floor scrubbed and big welcome wreaths of flowers ready to slip over the heads of Nellie, Herbert, Wild Rose and Susie as soon as he heard the car.

Then came six o'clock. Mrs. Campbell took the chicken pie out of the oven, wrapped a damp tea towel around the salad and put her big yellow mixing bowl over the coconut cake. Mr. Campbell separated the milk, fed the calves and kept his eye peeled on the road in from the highway.

Then seven o'clock came. Mrs. Campbell put the chicken pie back in the oven, peered anxiously at the salad and opened the canned peaches. Mr. Campbell, who by this time had changed his clothes and was all washed and combed, lit his pipe and went out on the back porch.

Then at last, far down the road, appeared the lights of a car, Sandy began to bark and Mr. Campbell called, "Mary Ann, Mary Ann, they're coming."

Mrs. Campbell smoothed her hair down with her hands, hung her apron behind the stove, checked the floor to be sure there wasn't a speck or a crumb on it and went out on the porch. Mr. Campbell put his arm around her and said, "I'm praying, too, honey."

Slowly the car crawled up the road. Mrs. Campbell's heart pounded thump, thump, thump and her mouth was so dry she couldn't swallow.

She said, "It's going to be awfully hard for me to be nice to that Mr. Remson."

He said, "Oh, that won't be hard once we have Nancy and Plum. Just remember that he's an old bachelor and doesn't know a thing about children."

She said, "But I keep thinking of him turning those babies over to that Mrs. Monday."

He said, "Well, at least it hasn't hurt them any. They are the prettiest, smartest, most well-behaved children I've ever seen."

She said, "That anybody has ever seen."

Then the car was at the door and Nancy and Plum were on the porch hugging and kissing the Campbells and shouting, "We're back. We're back!"

Mr. Remson looked pretty sheepish as he waddled up the steps and shook hands with the Campbells. He said, "That woman fooled me completely. Terrible creature. When we went up to get Nancy and Pamela, we found them locked in the attic and they haven't had a morsel of food since they left here."

Miss Waverly said, "Speaking of food, let me help you, Mary Ann. Where's an apron?"

Mrs. Campbell said, "Everything's ready. I baked you another chicken pie, Plum."

Plum said, "Oh, boy," and gave Mrs. Campbell another hug.

Nancy said, "Is there anything I can do to help?" Mrs. Campbell thought she sounded a little wistful, so she said, "Do you know what Angus said today when I told him I was going to bake a chicken pie? He said, 'It's going to be pretty hard to eat your cooking now that I've tasted Nancy's.'"

Nancy said, "Oh, Uncle Angus, you shouldn't talk like that!" But she looked very pleased.

Then they were all sitting at the kitchen table, even Danby, the chauffeur, eating chicken pie, hot biscuits, spring salad, pickled beets, coconut cake and canned peaches.

When Uncle John passed his plate for a third helping of chicken pie, Plum nudged Nancy and whispered, "I bet he'd like to live here, too."

After supper, while the grown people held a conference in the parlor, Nancy and Plum surprised Mrs. Campbell by washing the dishes and tidying up the kitchen. Nancy was just sweeping up the crumbs while Plum held the dustpan, when Mrs. Campbell came out to get a glass of water for Uncle John. She told the girls they shouldn't have bothered, kissed them and told them there were a few little surprises for them up on their bed.

They came down in a few minutes in their new blue jeans, T-shirts and tennis shoes, wearing their straw farmer hats, carrying the knife and the sewing box. The conference in the parlor was just breaking up and Miss Waverly was telling

Uncle John that she thought that prosecuting Mrs. Monday would be far too upsetting to the children. In her opinion the best thing to do was give Mrs. Monday a warning and then to help the children forget all about her and to start in fresh at the Campbells'.

Miss Appleby said that she thought that as long as the Campbells would not accept payment for Nancy and Plum's board, she thought Uncle John should put the money in the bank for their college education. She said, "You can send them clothes and books, the expensive toys such as sleds and bicycles, pay their dentist bills and give them music and dancing lessons."

Uncle John said, "Very well. Just send me a list of what you need and I'll send a check."

Plum said, "We don't need anything. Look at us. New jeanies, new shirts and *new shoes!*"

She lifted up her left foot and kissed her new red tennis shoe.

13

"Merry Christmas,
Everybody in the Whole World!"

IT WAS CHRISTMAS EVE. Big snowflakes fluttered slowly through the air like white feathers and made all of Heavenly Valley smooth and white and quiet and beautiful.

Tall fir trees stood up to their knees in the snow and their outstretched hands were heaped with it. Those that were bare of leaves wore soft white fur on their scrawny, reaching arms and all the stumps and low bushes had been turned into fat white cupcakes.

Mrs. Campbell sat in the rocking chair by the stove in the kitchen putting the finishing touches on Plum's angel costume. Nancy's was on the ironing board ready to be pressed.

As Mrs. Campbell worked, she hummed and rocked and took care that Penny's three kittens, who were playing around her feet, didn't get under the rockers.

Mr. Campbell came up on the back porch, stamped the snow off his boots, took off his cap and banged it against the house, slipped off his gloves and slapped them together, then took the broom and swept off the top of his boots and his knees. He came into the warm kitchen, hung his jacket, cap and mittens behind the stove and said to Mrs. Campbell, "Well, that's a load off my mind. Plum's Christmas present got here right on schedule. A beautiful little black filly with a white star on her forehead. I named her Noel. Nellie is so proud she is ready to bust."

Mrs. Campbell said, "Oh, Angus, how wonderful! Born Christmas Eve and named Noel. Plum will love that and just think, a horse of her very own. Well, I have Nancy's present all wrapped. I thought for a while I'd never finish ironing those little clothes. I certainly hope that I'm not just imagining that she will like the lady doll and trunk of clothes that my grandmother had when she was a little girl. The doll is still very pretty with real hair, eyelashes and eyebrows but the clothes are so old-fashioned. Hoop skirts and so many petticoats."

Mr. Campbell said, "You know Nancy will like that doll better than anything in the whole world. She'll like it because it is old-fashioned and because it has a trunk full of clothes."

Mrs. Campbell said, "Well, I certainly hope so. My heavens, that doll has everything. Little fans, necklaces, capes, bonnets, mitts, parasols and dozens of petticoats and dresses.

And that trunk is almost full size. Don't you think the girls should be back by now?"

Mr. Campbell said, "Oh, they'll be along in a minute. Cutting your first Christmas tree is a very important job and takes lots of picking and choosing. What are you making there?"

Mrs. Campbell said, "Plum's angel costume for the program at the schoolhouse. Nancy's is all finished. See!" She held up the long white satin dress and stretched out the gauzy wings.

Mr. Campbell said, "Gosh, Mary Ann, that's beautiful." He fingered the satin and said, "Where did you ever get such fine goods?"

Mrs. Campbell snapped off a thread between her teeth and said, "My wedding dress, that's where. For weeks those children have been talking about the program and their angel costumes and for weeks I've been wracking my brain trying to figure out what to make them out of. Then day before yesterday, I was up in the attic rummaging around in the old trunks and I came across my wedding dress, all wrapped in tissue paper and certainly as useless as a white elephant. I took it out and looked at it and I confess, Angus, I got very sentimental thinking about that day in June fifteen years ago. Then I said to myself, 'Listen, Mary Ann Campbell, one wedding is all you're ever going to have, and what earthly use to you is all that white satin and veiling?' Right then and there I knew what I was going to do."

Mr. Campbell leaned down and kissed her cheek and said, "I think angel costumes are the best use for your wedding dress I've ever heard of. What bothers me, Mary Ann, is the fact that this will be Nancy and Plum's first Christmas and I'm afraid we haven't enough for them. They know we don't have much money but after all they are only children and undoubtedly expect all kinds of miracles."

Mrs. Campbell said, "I've thought of the same thing a million times, but I have decided that to Nancy and Plum the most wonderful thing of all is that they have a home and a family on Christmas. Stuffing the turkey, getting and trimming their own Christmas tree, going to the school program in the sleigh, these angel costumes, having Old Tom and Miss Waverly for Christmas dinner, the presents they had Uncle John buy for the other children at Mrs. Monday's, are the important things to those children. Not expensive gifts. Anyway, I sent away and got them each a pair of party shoes and I have made them each a new dress. Plum's is cherry-red velveteen and Nancy's is sky blue. I also got plenty of little things for their stockings."

Mr. Campbell said, "So did I."

There was a loud knocking on the door. Thinking it was the children, Mrs. Campbell quickly gathered up the angel costumes and hid them under her apron. Mr. Campbell opened the door. It wasn't Nancy and Plum. It was Danby, Uncle John's chauffeur, standing on the porch beside two beautiful sleds and a huge box.

"Come in, come in," Mrs. Campbell said. But Danby said no, he'd left his car down the road and he had a big load of packages to deliver to Mrs. Monday's.

"Oh, Danby," said Aunt Mary Ann. "Did Mr. Remson get everything on the list?"

"Got the list right here," said Danby, pulling off one of his heavy woolen gloves with his teeth, and fumbling in his inside pocket. When he found it he read it off to Mrs. Campbell—

> **Eunice**—large girl doll—blond curls—blue eyes—real
>   eyelashes and eyebrows.
>   blue coat and bonnet with fur.
>   nightgown.
>   bathrobe, bedroom slippers.
>   4 school dresses.
>   2 pinafores.
>   2 party dresses.
>   ski suit.
>   skis.
>   roller-skating costume.
>   roller skates.
>   ice-skating costume.
>   ice skates.
>   Girl Scout uniform.
>   Camp Fire Girl uniform.
>   ballet dress.
>   toe shoes.
>   cowgirl set.
>   2 sweaters.
>   play coat.

jeans.

plaid shirt.

Allan—electric train—large size with lots of tunnels— signals—stations—switches.

Todd—same.

David—same.

Tommy—cowboy suit.

two-gun holster with guns.

lariat.

real cowboy boots.

hat.

pocketknife with five blades.

Mary—cowgirl outfit.

two-gun holster with guns.

lariat.

real cowboy boots.

hat.

pocketknife with five blades.

Sally—same.

Evangeline—same.

The rest of the little boys had sleds and new mittens, a cap and a sweater and all the children big candy canes—books— large boxes of crayons and coloring books.

When Danby finished, the Campbells said, "Oh, Danby, how wonderful! What a thrilling Christmas this will be for those poor little souls. Imagine that poor little David getting nothing but two suits of long underwear last Christmas."

Danby said, "Mr. Remson told me to deliver the boxes to Old Tom and have him distribute the gifts. They are all wrapped real fancy."

"How wonderful," said Mrs. Campbell.

"All the credit goes to Nancy and Plum," Mr. Campbell said. "If they weren't such unselfish children they could have had all that money spent on presents for them."

"Oh," said Danby, "their uncle said that he appreciated their unselfishness but he just sent along these sleds and this box for them. Well, I must get along. Mr. Remson told me to give any of the kids that wanted, and were going home, a ride to the city."

"How nice," said Mrs. Campbell, "and how much pleasanter than riding on the train with Mrs. Monday and that horrid little Marybelle. Well, a merry, merry Christmas to you, Danby, and thank you so much for driving way out here in the snow."

"'Twasn't anything," Danby said. "Merry Christmas to you all, too," he called as he hurried down the steps and disappeared into the snowstorm.

"Just wait until Nancy and Plum hear that Uncle John got everything on their list. They'll be the happiest children in Heavenly Valley. Now, Angus, you hurry and put on your jacket and take those sleds down to the barn and hide them. I'll just see what's in this other box."

Mr. Campbell slipped on his jacket, grabbed up the sleds and ran down to the barn. As he opened the door, he could hear Nancy and Plum's voices down the lane.

Mrs. Campbell spread newspapers on the floor, brought in the huge box and cut the strings. As she raised the lid, yards and yards of white tissue paper fell to the floor. Carefully she reached in and lifted out first a beautiful little dark green coat trimmed with gray squirrel, a darling little hat and a gray squirrel muff. "For my Nancy," she said, her eyes bright with happiness.

Then a beautiful little bright red coat trimmed with gray squirrel, a darling little hat and a gray squirrel muff. "For my Plum," Mrs. Campbell said, a smile lighting up her whole face.

Then black patent-leather party shoes, silk socks, heaps of lacy underwear and two party dresses, with the fullest, whirliest skirts ever made. Dark green taffeta for Nancy, dark blue taffeta for Plum.

There were also two packages for Old Tom, one a very large box, two beautifully wrapped silver and green packages for Miss Waverly and, to Aunt Mary Ann's astonishment, a small box marked "Mrs. Campbell from a very grateful Mr. Remson" and a small box marked "Mr. Campbell from a very grateful Mr. Remson."

"My goodness, my goodness, what a Christmas this is going to be," she said. Then hearing Nancy and Plum on the back porch, she grabbed up the packages for Old Tom, Miss Waverly, Angus and herself and stuffed them in the front hall coat closet; snatched up all the clothes, ran upstairs and laid them out on the girls' bed.

When she came down, Mr. Campbell had set the box on

the back porch and was helping Nancy and Plum put up their tree.

Both children had snow on their caps, their shoulders, their mittens and galoshes and had tracked big gobs of it into the parlor but Mrs. Campbell hugged them, kissed their cold pink cheeks and said, "What a beautiful tree!"

Plum said, "We walked for about a hundred miles looking for a perfect one."

Nancy said, "See, this one even has little cones on it!"

Mr. Campbell said, "I've got the standard all ready. While you take off your wraps and brush the snow off you, I'll put it up. Then you can decorate it."

Nancy said, "Oh, Plum, look how much snow we brought in and on the clean floor, too."

Mrs. Campbell said, "Nobody can bring in a Christmas tree without tracking in a little snow. Now go out on the porch and sweep each other off and hurry because I've got to put up your hair in curlers."

As soon as the back door closed, she told Mr. Campbell about the beautiful new clothes Uncle John had sent.

Mr. Campbell said, "Golly, that's fine, Mary Ann, but what about the dresses and new shoes you have for them?"

Mrs. Campbell said, "I'll just not say anything about them and then a little later on when these shoes have gotten kind of scuffy and they've worn their new dresses quite a few times, I'll bring mine out."

Mr. Campbell said, "Sure, that's a fine idea. I think that

two pairs of new party shoes right now would be too much for Plum anyhow. Probably send her out of her head."

They both laughed. As soon as Nancy and Plum had hung their coats, caps and mittens behind the stove to dry, Mrs. Campbell put their hair up in curlers, then sent them up to their room to see the surprise. They racketed up the stairs like streaks. Then Mr. and Mrs. Campbell, who were following, heard loud Oh's and Ah's and squeals of pure delight. When the Campbells reached their room, the children were trying on the new coats, hats and muffs.

Plum looked in the mirror and said, "Wow, I look just like a princess, even with these curlers in my hair."

Nancy stood quietly stroking her muff. Mrs. Campbell said, "Isn't the coat beautiful, Nancy? And it fits just perfectly."

Nancy said, "Oh, Aunt Mary Ann, I'm so happy I feel funny. I keep thinking 'All this can't be happening to me.' Pretty soon I'll wake up and know that it was only another one of my dreams."

Plum said, "Wow, Nancy, come and look how full the skirts on our party dresses are. And *new party shoes*! I didn't even see them before. Oh, Nancy, Nancy, look, black patent-leather slippers just like Marybelle's." Plum held one of the slippers up and rubbed its smooth shininess against her cheek.

Nancy picked up her slippers carefully, as though they were crown jewels, stroked the toes, felt the straps and her lips trembled as she said, "I just don't think I could hold any more happiness right now. My heart feels like it's going to burst."

Mrs. Campbell hugged her and said, "Well, I don't want

you bursting and spoiling your new coat, but I've got two more surprises for you. The first is that Danby drove in a few minutes ago to tell us that Uncle John got every single thing on the list and he's delivering them to Old Tom right now. He couldn't wait to see you because he had to get the presents to the Boarding Home before Mrs. Monday and the children left for the train."

"Did he get Eunice's doll and the clothes?" Nancy asked.

"Exactly as you ordered it," Mrs. Campbell said.

"And the electric trains?" Plum said.

"All three of them," Mrs. Campbell said.

"Oh, wow," Plum said, "I almost wish I was over there just so's I could see their faces."

"It wouldn't do you any good to be there," Mrs. Campbell said, "because Danby is going to take as many of the children as he can into town in his car and they won't even know about the presents until he drops them off at their home. Then when they get out he'll give them the present."

"What about the ones who have to go on the train?" Plum asked.

"Old Tom is putting their presents with their suitcases," Aunt Mary Ann said.

"Oh, poor Eunice will have to go on the train," Nancy said, "because her aunt lives way beyond the city. She won't care though when she sees that doll."

"What about the presents for Old Tom—the 'lectric lantern and the new mackinaw?" Plum asked.

"I've got 'em right downstairs in the coat closet," said Mrs. Campbell. "We'll give them to him when he comes for dinner tomorrow."

"What about the violet things for Miss Waverly?" Nancy asked. "The perfume and bath salts and soap and all?"

"Also in the hall closet," said Aunt Mary Ann. "Not only that, but your Uncle John sent a present for Uncle Angus and one for me. Now enough talking. You girls go downstairs and start trimming the tree and I'll get my other surprise ready. My goodness, we'll have to hurry, too. I've supper to get, you have baths to take, we'll have to leave here by seven and it's almost five o'clock right now."

The fire in the fireplace snapped and crackled and the flames were gloriously reflected on the ornaments as Nancy and Plum carefully hung them on the fragrant branches.

They were almost through. Even though they had done it all themselves they agreed that it was the most gorgeous Christmas tree in the world.

Nancy said, "As soon as we finish, let's go up and get our presents for Aunt Mary Ann and Uncle Angus and put them under the tree."

Plum said, "I'll run up and get them while you put on those last two birds." The little birds were an iridescent blue with clear spun glass tails and Nancy attached them to the very end of the branches where they'd catch the firelight. Then, she stood back and looked and looked at the Christmas tree.

When Plum came in with the packages, she said, "You know, Plum, it's really better we never did have a Christmas tree at Mrs. Monday's."

Plum said, "Why, for heaven's sake?"

"Because," Nancy said, "having never had one we didn't know what we were missing."

Plum said, "My presents look awful—like I'd slept with them."

Nancy said, "No they don't. They look nice. Here, I'll tie a better bow for you on Aunt Mary Ann's."

Plum said, "Do you think she's going to like those guest towels I made her? I got them so dirty when I was embroidering them that they look as if they have already been used."

Nancy said, "They're just beautiful, Plum, and you did a very nice job on your cross-stitching."

Plum said, "Nice job if you don't look at the back. How come I have so many millions of threads and big knots on the back of mine and yours are so smooth?"

Nancy said, "Oh, that's just because I've been sewing a lot longer than you have. Anyway, who looks at the back?"

Plum said, "Do you think we have enough presents for Aunt Mary Ann and Uncle Angus? They're so wonderful to us and I love them so much I'd like to give them a million dollars."

Nancy said, "They'd much rather have these things we made ourselves. Miss Waverly says that things you make show a lot more thought and love than things you just go in and buy. After all, anybody with money can buy presents."

Plum said, "Let's see, I made Aunt Mary Ann those dirty guest towels and that pincushion that looks like it has the mumps. Then I made Uncle Angus that pipe rack that's all splintery on one end and knitted him that scarf that has so many dropped stitches in it, it looks like lace."

Nancy, who was laughing, said, "Now you stop talking that way. I saw all your presents and they're just fine. Anyway, I'm not sure Aunt Mary Ann will like the apron and pot holders I made her or that Uncle Angus will like the bed socks I crocheted him. But I think they will."

Plum said, "Oh, look at the kittens climbing the Christmas tree. They think we brought it in just for them. Hey, Dasher, don't you knock those ornaments off. Look, Nancy, at Cupid peering out from behind those branches."

Mrs. Campbell called from the kitchen, "Time for your bubble baths and another surprise."

The children whisked out to the kitchen. There, spread out on the ironing board, were the two angel costumes to wear in the program. They were even lovelier than the ones Nancy had pretended for them!

Nancy said, "Plum, just imagine how we're going to look standing by the Christmas tree singing the carols. People will probably think we are real angels."

Mrs. Campbell said, "And they won't be far wrong. Now you girls scoot in and take your baths. I've put your new underwear and party shoes in there and you can eat supper in your bathrobes. I've made oyster stew, so hurry. The lamp's already in there and I've lit the heater."

Nancy and Plum lay back in their mountains of bubbles and the round red eye of the coal-oil heater looked down at them from the ceiling. The bathroom was not very warm and smelled pungently of kerosene and imitation gardenia but to Nancy and Plum it was the personification of luxury.

Plum said, "This bubble bath is so much fun, I almost wish we didn't have to go to the program."

Nancy said, "Well, we do, and you'd better scrub your elbows. They're awfully dirty."

Plum said, "I can't scrub them. They're both skinned and they hurt."

Nancy said, "Well, I don't think that white gauzy angel wings over jet-black elbows is going to look very pretty."

Plum said, "I'll keep my arms down at my sides."

Nancy said, "We're supposed to keep our hands pressed together in front of us like we're praying."

Plum said, "Well, I'll pretend my wings have black spots on them like butterflies' do."

Nancy said, "Now, Plum, you can't do that. You'd disappoint Aunt Mary Ann."

So Plum scrubbed her elbows but she flinched and winced and told Nancy she was almost fainting with the pain.

After they had rubbed themselves dry with the big rough towels, Nancy and Plum put on their new ruffly underwear, silk socks and then, joy of joys, slipped their feet into the stiff newness of their patent-leather slippers.

Plum took a step. "Gosh, Nancy," she said, "they're as slippery as ice. Even the soles must be polished."

214

Nancy said, "You don't suppose that walking in them will wrinkle the toes, do you?"

Plum said, "Well, I'm not going to take a chance. I'm going to walk like this," and she slid out of the bathroom and down the hall toward the kitchen like a skater with stiff knees. Nancy followed her, swinging her stiff legs forward like a windup doll.

Mr. Campbell watching them come into the kitchen said, "My gosh, that bubble bath must have been too strong. Look, Mary Ann, they're all stiffened up."

Plum said, "It's not that. We don't want to bend our new shoes. They might wrinkle."

Mrs. Campbell said, "My goodness, Angus, anybody at all knows that you have to walk stiff-legged in party shoes. Now everybody sit down and eat their soup."

Nancy and Plum were just choking down the last of their oyster stew when they heard sleigh bells and horses' hooves, the stamping of snowy feet on the back porch and then loud knocking on the door.

With round scared eyes they looked at each other. Plum said, "I'm afraid to have you go to the door, Uncle Angus."

Nancy said, "I knew we were too happy."

"Nonsense," said Mrs. Campbell. "Probably a neighbor wanting help with a new calf or something. Hurry, Angus, and see who it is."

The knocking was repeated before Mr. Campbell could cross the kitchen. "Hold your horses," he said as he swung open the door. There on the back porch stood Old Tom and beside him, her eyes swollen shut with crying and still gulping with sobs, stood Eunice.

Old Tom said, "She didn't tell this little one until this afternoon that she wasn't going home for Christmas. Got the letter from her aunt 'most a week ago, but she didn't tell her till this afternoon. She's been out in the barn cryin' ever since. Thought maybe you'd have room for one more over here."

Mr. Campbell said, "You bet we have, come right in, both of you."

Mrs. Campbell said, "You poor little mite," and clasped Eunice to her warm toasty-smelling bosom.

Nancy and Plum rushed over and hugged Eunice, too. Nancy said, "Oh, Eunice, I'm glad you didn't go home. You can sleep in our big feather bed with us and we'll have Christmas together."

Plum said, "And you can go to the program with us tonight."

Eunice said, "I can't go to the program. My dress is dirty and my shoes are soaking wet."

Nancy said, "You can wear my new dress. It's silk and has a big whirly skirt. I'll wear a school dress."

Mrs. Campbell said, "That's sweet of you, Nancy, dear, but it won't be necessary. I have a new dress and new party shoes for Eunice."

"How could you?" asked Plum. "I mean, how did you know Eunice was coming?"

"I guess an angel must have told me," said Mrs. Campbell.

216

"Now, while I get Eunice's clothes, you girls help her out of those wet things and fix Tom and her some hot oyster stew."

Nancy fixed the stew while Plum took off Eunice's soggy worn-out shoes and soggy thin coat, then held them up and in an exact imitation of Mrs. Monday said, "You see, deah, deah Mr. Remson, these lovely, lovely garments and these beautiful brand new shoes? Well, this horrible little child, this greedy, selfish little Eunice isn't satisfied with them and is demanding something bettah." Eunice and Nancy laughed and laughed and then Aunt Mary Ann came in with the sky-blue velvet dress, brand new underwear and socks, and the new party shoes. Nancy and Plum shrieked with joy, but Eunice couldn't believe it. Shyly she stroked the soft velvet dress, but she didn't offer to take any of the things.

Mrs. Campbell said, "They're for you, dear. Here."

Eunice said, "Are you sure, Mrs. Campbell? Are you very sure?"

"I'm as sure as I'm standing here," Mrs. Campbell said. "Just try them on and see, but first you've got to eat your soup and take a bath. Plum, you go in and run the water in the tub and be sure and put in plenty of bubble bath. Nancy, you put Eunice's shoes and clean underwear in the bathroom and take her dress upstairs. Now everybody scat or we'll be late for the program."

"The program," Nancy said. "What about Eunice? She hasn't got an angel costume."

Eunice said, "Oh, Nancy, it doesn't make any difference.

217

Only you and Plum are the angels. The rest of us just wear regular dresses."

Mrs. Campbell said, "Are you sure, honey? Because I could take one of my white petticoats and fix you something."

"Oh, no, Mrs. Campbell," Eunice said, "I'm not supposed to wear an angel dress and, anyway, even if I was, I don't think I'd want to. Not with that beautiful blue velvet one to wear."

While Eunice was taking her bath, Mrs. Campbell helped Nancy and Plum into their taffeta dresses with the whirly skirts, took down their rag curlers and curled their hair around her finger.

"What are you going to do about Eunice's hair?" Plum wanted to know. "She said she washed it this morning, but of course old muscley fingers Mrs. Monday braided it into braids as hard as rocks."

Mrs. Campbell said, "You hold your head still, young lady, or I'll braid your hair. There, that's better. Now, about Eunice. The dress, underwear and party shoes I gave her were really meant for Nancy. I made you girls each new dresses and sent away for the slippers before I knew that Uncle John was sending them to you. Of course we won't say a word to Eunice and after Christmas I'll make Nancy another dress and get her some more shoes. It was just pure luck about the dress and shoes, but I'm afraid I can't produce curls. Not this late anyway."

"Oh, it won't make any difference anyway," Nancy said. "We'll undo the braids and brush out her hair and it will be all wavy and will look beautiful. Golly, wasn't it lucky about the dress? It's just beautiful, Aunty Mary Ann. Really a lot prettier than this one Uncle John sent."

"That's just because it's the color of your eyes, Nancy," Mrs. Campbell said.

"What color is mine?" Plum asked.

"Cherry-red," Mrs. Campbell said.

"Just the color of your eyes," Nancy said, and she and Plum laughed.

When Aunty Mary Ann finished her hair, Plum whirled around and around until her skirt stood out like a parasol and her curls stretched out long and sprang back like watch springs. "Now," she said, "the only things that Marybelle has that we don't have are near-together eyes, a squeaky voice and a big crabby aunt."

Nancy laughed, but Aunt Mary Ann said, "You might have a big crabby aunt, too, if you don't stop shaking your head and trying to make your curls come out."

Plum gave her a big hug and said, "You couldn't be crabby, you don't know how."

Mrs. Campbell kissed her and said, "Now scoot upstairs and bring down the coats while I finish Nancy. Bring Nancy's blue Sunday-School coat for Eunice and in on my bed is a little white fur muff and tippet I had when I was a little girl. Bring those."

"What's a tippet?" Plum asked.

"A little fur scarf," Mrs. Campbell said. "Now scat."

Just then Eunice came out of the bathroom. Her eyes were only a little swollen now and even that didn't show, they were so happy and shining. Her cheeks were bright pink and she was wearing the new ruffly petticoat and her new party shoes.

She was walking stiff-legged, of course, but Aunt Mary Ann knelt down, punched the toes of the shoes and pronounced them a perfect fit.

"Now," she said, giving Eunice a hug and a kiss, "you look good enough to eat. Now hurry upstairs and put on that new dress. It's almost time to go."

As soon as Eunice had left, Nancy said, "What about the doll? Where is it? And will there be anything else under the Christmas tree for Eunice?"

"The doll," Old Tom said, "is out in the back of my sleigh. I'll just duck out and get it now."

When he came in, Mrs. Campbell said, "Here, give it to me. I'll hide it in the hall closet." When she came back she had two little presents for her and Angus from Uncle John. She said, "Here, Angus, let's open these now. We can't be the only ones without anything new. And you, too, Tom, you go out and get that big box for you from Nancy and Plum."

Uncle John had sent Mr. and Mrs. Campbell each a beautiful wrist watch. A little round gold one with a thin gold bracelet for Mrs. Campbell and a larger gold one with a leather strap for Mr. Campbell. They were the first watches either of them had ever had and they were so thrilled they had tears in their eyes. Then Mr. Campbell looked at the back of his and found engraved on it "To Uncle Angus from Plum and Nancy." Mrs. Campbell turned hers over and found "To Aunt Mary Ann from Plum and Nancy." They both kissed Nancy and Plum and then Old Tom opened his present and saw his mackinaw and he kissed them and thanked them and then everybody was laughing and squealing and jumping around until Mrs. Campbell looked at the clock and saw that it was ten minutes after seven.

"Oh, my goodness," she said. "We've got to hurry. Here, Eunice, this little white fur scarf and muff is for you. Come here and I'll fix it. Now you look just like a princess except for your hair. Heavens, I forgot your hair. Quick, slip out of your coat while I start unbraiding. Nancy, you do the other braid and, Plum, you hand me the brush."

In a few minutes Eunice's thick brown hair hung down her back in shiny rippling waves. "Now you really do look like a princess," Nancy said.

At last they were ready. The angel costumes were laid out flat in a box, carefully wrapped in tissue paper, and stowed in the back of the sleigh. Nancy and Plum and Eunice were resplendent in their new coats, hats and muffs. Aunt Mary Ann and Uncle Angus were bundled up in their regular coats and scarves, but wearing their new watches. Old Tom had shed his old dusty jacket and had on his new warm red-plaid wool mackinaw. The sleigh was at the door and Old Horse and Herbert were snorting and stamping in the cold.

As Mr. Campbell tucked the robes around the children and clucked to the horses, Nancy said, "Remember, Plum, last Christmas when we said that someday we'd be going to the Christmas entertainment in a sleigh?"

Plum said, "Certainly, I remember. I said I'd be driving."

Mr. Campbell handed her the reins. Plum slapped them on the horses' backs and shouted, "Merry Christmas, Old Horse and Herbert."

The horses stepped along smartly, the runners of the sleigh hissed in the snow, the sleigh bells trilled shrilly and Eunice called out, "Merry Christmas, School Program, here we come."

Then Nancy, her hand tight in Mrs. Campbell's warm comforting hand, looked around her and called out, "Merry Christmas, horses. Merry Christmas, Heavenly Valley. Merry Christmas, everybody in the whole world!"

THE END

Betty MacDonald was born Anne Elizabeth Campbell Bard in Boulder, Colorado, in 1908. The daughter of a mining engineer, she spent her early years in some of the mining towns of Idaho, Montana, and Mexico. When she was nine, her father took the family—his wife and five children—to Seattle, where Betty lived until shortly after her marriage.

Among her books for children are *Nancy and Plum*, originally published in 1952, and the beloved classics *Mrs. Piggle-Wiggle*, *Mrs. Piggle-Wiggle's Magic*, *Mrs. Piggle-Wiggle's Farm*, and *Hello, Mrs. Piggle-Wiggle*.

Mary GrandPré has illustrated thirteen children's books, including, most recently, *Carnival of the Animals* and several chapter books. She interrupted her work on picture books to illustrate all of the Harry Potter books. That assignment finished, she welcomed the chance to be involved with *Nancy and Plum*, and is currently working on more children's books and exploring personal paintings on a larger scale in the studio. She lives in Florida. You can visit her at marygrandpre.com.

When Jeanne Birdsall was young, she promised herself she'd be a writer someday—so she could write books for children to discover and enjoy, just as she did in her local library. In fact, she is especially honored to work on *Nancy and Plum* because she distinctly remembers reading each and every entry in Betty MacDonald's Mrs. Piggle-Wiggle series as a young, impressionable girl.

Jeanne is the author of *The Penderwicks*, which won the National Book Award for Young People's Literature, and its follow-ups, *The Penderwicks on Gardam Street* and *The Penderwicks at Point Mouette*. She lives in Northampton, Massachusetts, with her husband, three nutty cats, and a dog named Cagney. You can find out more about Jeanne (and her animal friends) at her website, jeannebirdsall.com.

YEARLING!

Looking for more great books to read?
Check these out!

- *All-of-a-Kind Family* by Sydney Taylor
- *Are You There God? It's Me, Margaret* by Judy Blume
- *Blubber* by Judy Blume
- *The City of Ember* by Jeanne DuPrau
- *Crash* by Jerry Spinelli
- *The Girl Who Threw Butterflies* by Mick Cochrane
- *The Gypsy Game* by Zilpha Keatley Snyder
- *Heart of a Shepherd* by Rosanne Parry
- *The King of Mulberry Street* by Donna Jo Napoli
- *The Mailbox* by Audrey Shafer

- *Me, Mop, and the Moondance Kid* by Walter Dean Myers
- *My One Hundred Adventures* by Polly Horvath
- *The Penderwicks* by Jeanne Birdsall
- *Skellig* by David Almond
- *Soft Rain* by Cornelia Cornelissen
- *Stealing Freedom* by Elisa Carbone
- *Toys Go Out* by Emily Jenkins
- *A Traitor Among the Boys* by Phyllis Reynolds Naylor
- *Two Hot Dogs with Everything* by Paul Haven
- *When My Name Was Keoko* by Linda Sue Park